SURRENDERED III
FORGIVENESS

BY

PEGGY PATRICK

ENDORSEMENTS

The Surrendered Novels are a series of books full of love, forgiveness and healing. Each book contains characters that are easy to fall in love with and situations in life that are easy to relate to. The love stories thoughout the Surrendered novels are so pure and beautiful! The Surrendered novels are true love stories, the way God meant love stories to be!
*****Amanda

I have read all 3 books and I love them all. The story, the connection. Wonderful books. After I started #3, I could not put it down. We went to some friends

house New Year's Eve and there were about 50 friends gathered there. I have a kindle on my phone and I was constantly opening it and reading. My husband asked me, "What are you doing?" I said, "reading." He was like, "Rose, there are a bunch of our friends here. Don't you want to mingle and visit?" I was like, "Yes, but I can't stop reading. I want to know what is gonna happen." He just laughed at me!! It was a very good book. I couldn't put it down.
*****Rose

Easy to read, couldn't put it down. I have read all three Surrendered books and enjoyed each one. Great work Peggy Patrick.
*****Ann

For my grandchildren, who are the light of this Meme's life:

SURRENDERED III

FORGIVENESS

CHAPTER ONE

"No, puppy…don't do it!" Kaitlyn Grace braked and veered her Toyota Camry off the highway sharply to the right, but the shoulder wasn't much. She couldn't go far enough.

Thump!

"Oh, no!" She swallowed the urge to be sick as she steered her car off the road as far as possible and threw it in park. A quick glance showed her that no other vehicles were in sight as she jumped out and ran back several yards to where the little brown furry lump lay unmoving. She knew the dog was dead, but she couldn't leave it lying there like that.

She squatted down beside it and glanced quickly in both directions for oncoming traffic. "I'm sorry, little guy," she whispered as she slid her hands beneath the still, warm body and lifted it into her arms. There was no blood. It appeared the injuries were internal. She laid the little dog on the back seat and got back behind the wheel. She made a U-turn across the two lane and headed back home. She had one old four-legged family member buried beneath a big oak tree beside her barn. The least she could do is give this little unlucky pup a decent place to be buried.

Before she had driven a half mile, a pitiful little whimper came from the back seat. A startled glance back confirmed it—*He's alive!* Without a second thought, she whipped over and waited for the road to clear and did another U-turn to head back toward Joplin and the only animal hospital on her end of the Missouri city.

It had been several years since Kaitlyn had had a reason to stop at the vet clinic. She pulled up into the parking area and felt her heart sink. The mixture of guilt and shame that stabbed her heart would have overwhelmed her except for the cry coming from her back seat that took precedence over the sudden rush of hurtful memories.

She went inside and explained the situation. Within a minute, two young female employees went out and carried the little patient back inside on a backboard.

Kaitlyn left her address with instructions for them to send her a bill. Before she got fully out of the front door, she overheard a young woman loudly announce to another worker across the office, "Dr. Kane's supplies are boxed and ready to be shipped."

Hearing that name jolted her heart and stopped her feet. She turned around in the open doorway and unlocked her voice box after the second try. "Is that Dr. Les Kane that used to work here?"

The girl looked up and smiled. "Yes...I think it is. But that was before my time here."

Kaitlyn tried to sound nonchalant. "Oh, so where did he get off to?" She hoped her trembling was not visible.

"Uh, let's see here." She turned the box on the counter around. "Jackson, Wyoming—Double OO Ranch. At least that's where these supplies are being shipped to. Was he your vet?"

Yes, he was MY vet and the biggest mistake I've ever made in my life!

She nodded and headed back home to the ranch, shelving her original plans for shopping in Joplin that day. She had simply lost the heart for it.

In truth, Kaitlyn hadn't had a heart for much of anything the past few years. One foot in front of the other was a chore at times.

Somehow, she had managed to hold herself together after her entire family had deserted her. And Les Kane. He was the only one who hadn't deserted. She had forced him to leave and made it unwaveringly clear that he was not welcome in her life. Ever! She realized even before the dust cleared that she had made a terrible mistake.

But she couldn't go to her fiancé, the love of her life, to try and fix her mistake. Les had disappeared. His furnished apartment was emptied of his clothes and few personal effects. He was gone.

Kaitlyn pulled into her driveway and turned off the engine. She sat behind the steering wheel and moved her gaze over the grounds of her ranch that had been her home for close to three decades. It seemed she had moved around this ranch like a life-sized puppet with an unseen force pulling her strings. She grew up with one sibling, Wade, who was five years younger.

Kaitlyn was the one to mimic her father's footsteps, shadowing him around the horse barn. She felt loved because he was there with her and now and then let her ride a horse. When she was five, little brother, Wade, was born and everything changed. Her memories were vague now. All she could remember was how lonely she was and even wishing her name was Wade, instead of Kaitlyn. She recognized how different girls were from boys and decided in her adolescent mind that being given second place to baby brother was just part of that difference.

That belief was her survival within her family unit, until she was forced to admit the truth when Wade was diagnosed with brain cancer and died only two months later at age twenty. The snowball effect of her brother's death gave sudden and painful clarity to what she had tried to ignore. She didn't measure up.

Immediately after Wade's funeral service, Kaitlyn's mother, Rebecca Grace, drove away from the ranch and was never seen nor heard from again. And from that day forward her dad, Jason, acted as though Kaitlyn didn't exist.

No one existed for Jason Grace except Mae-Belle.

For years, Kaitlyn tried everything she knew to be somebody, even a stand-in for Wade in her father's life. But it seemed Mae-Belle had all the bases covered.

A week after the funeral, Kaitlyn had discovered a hand scribbled note laying open on her father's desk in his study. In her brother's weakened handwriting, he had asked his dad to take care of his beloved dog, Mae-Belle. Jason's grief for his son was only assuaged by the presence of the nine year old part collie, part mutt that Wade had picked up on a lonely back road when she was barely a year old. Jason didn't seem to be overly concerned that his wife had vanished. But Kaitlyn continued to hope that one day he might snap out of it. That never happened, but Dr. Les Kane happened. A chill shivered through Kaitlyn just before her eyes filled and burned with hot salt water.

"Les." His name came out in an agonized whisper.

She had been angry, hurt. Not so much at Les for what happened, but at Wade for dying, at her mother for dissolving into thin air and at her dad for worshipping his dead son's dog. And at the withheld love from her family that wasn't attainable no matter how hard she worked to get it.

What did she do? She struck out at one who *did* love her. She had twisted her engagement ring off her finger and bounced it off his face, screaming at him to disappear and never come back.

Both hands now gripped the steering wheel so hard her palms were burning. She dropped her head down onto the tops of her hands in sheer agony.

She remembered how she had gone to Les's apartment to beg his forgiveness, but he was gone. He never went back to the animal clinic where he worked. He was just—gone. Her emotions were suddenly raw and bleeding at the memory that she'd so carefully closed away all this time.

"Oh God, please." She got out of her car holding her stomach against the new surge of unbearable loneliness that enveloped her. She didn't want to go through this gut wrenching hurt again.

She walked briskly toward the empty barn that once was a busy and exciting equine training facility. But after her father's death three years ago, she closed the barn along with her self-respect. Life had become pointless.

Just then, Kaitlyn realized she was standing beside Mae-Belle's elaborately marked grave at the entrance to the riding arena. That had been the little dog's favorite spot to lounge during work days.

Shame dropped her to her knees beside the weed covered, rectangular mound of earth. She traced the writing on the headstone with her finger, *Mae-Belle Grace, Beloved Friend*, then worked slowly and methodically pulling the green blades of grass and weeds out of the grave spot.

It had been an accident—a careless mistake that, once made, couldn't be called back. She recalled that day when she entered the barn and found Les on his knees frantically trying to revive Mae-Belle. He had wormed several horses in the barn with tubes of paste and had accidentally shot the medicine from one tube out onto the concrete alleyway of the barn. After finishing up, he'd come to clean up the spilled paste, but Mae-Belle had already discovered it and licked it up. It poisoned her and nothing could be done. Les knew the worm paste was lethal to dogs, but didn't think until it was too late.

But it had been Jason's reaction that triggered Kaitlyn's breaking point. She watched her father discover the scene in the barn, saw him fall on top of Mae-Belle's still, warm body and moan in grief for his beloved son all over again. It all came crashing in on Kaitlyn until she reacted without a sane thought to temper the situation. Her engagement ring hit Les square in the face. And then he was gone.

Two weeks later, Jason Grace went to bed and died in his sleep.

It had been three years and time had helped bury some of her bad memories. But she did vividly remember the last time she saw Les' face—the heart-crushing pain in his huge beautiful brown eyes—the one image imprinted in her mind that she would never forget. And it was that embedded picture that she believed was the final blow that caused her to experience the most traumatic and life-altering circumstance of her life. It was the reason, she knew, even now as she knelt beside Mae-Belle's grave, that she had to try and find Les Kane. He had a right to know.

She hadn't seen or heard from him in all of these years. Maybe he had someone special. Maybe he was married. She contemplated calling the Double OO Ranch in Wyoming to see what she could find out, but decided—no. She needed to make the trip there and find him. This was the last thing on her short list of necessary *To Do's*. She had created this list, with the help of her counselor, during the last week of a six-month rehab at a Christian facility, Hope's Ranch, located in the hill country of southwest Texas.

Her two best girlfriends had begged her to go there. *Just give it thirty days. You've been through so much devastation and their success rate at restoring broken lives is phenomenal,* was their argument. Personally, she hadn't had enough presence of mind to have an argument after the last horrific loss that had taken her to the emotional end of herself.

Lisa and Valerie, best friends from school days, drove her there one week later, where one month turned into six. During that time, she was taken back to view her life with painful, but healing clarity. Both of her parents had been victimized in different ways as children. She had known bits and pieces of things about them, but never really recognized the emotional damage they must have carried with them into their adult lives. She had wondered how two people that grew up in different households, in different cities and both having suffered similar abuses, could find each other the way her parents did. And it all ended so horribly. That seemed like an abuse in itself. Finally, satisfied that she had given little Mae-Belle's place due respect, she stood up and breathed deeply of the fresh September chill in the air. She loved fall. She had spent fall and winter at Hope's Ranch in Texas two years ago. Since then, her favorite time of year began with the first hint of a crisp breeze. She turned her face upward and offered a silent praise to God.

It had been two weeks since Kaitlyn found out where Les went and she couldn't put this off any longer. Restlessness had been building the past days until she couldn't get a decent night's sleep.

With two suitcases, boots and a winter coat piled into the back seat of her black Camry, she drove 4 miles to the florist shop then back to the cemetery located on the farthest corner of the Grace ranch.   Her family was all buried beside each other there.

Before leaving town, she placed vases of white roses in front of three headstones, lingering a while beside the last one. She had already made her peace with each one—forgiving and asking for forgiveness. It was part of her healing process that she had learned in rehab. She was genuinely ready for that part, but was still amazed at the heavy burden that had lifted off of her afterward.

She had given her life to Jesus Christ at Hope's Ranch. A huge weight left her then, but she still had her part to do in order to become totally free. She knew she was forgiven. That was a done deal. But she needed to make restitution where she could, for her sake.

So, she had one more stop to make—The Double OO Ranch in Jackson, Wyoming.

Well, okay. Two more stops. She hadn't received a bill for the little unlucky dog she had run over. He probably didn't live, but she needed to stop and find out what she owed.

Les Kane stepped from his truck and made a run for it through the driving rain storm, slamming the door behind him. He carried his *puppy delivering* stuff packed into a small tote, the wind trying to claim it before he could get inside the barn at High Point Dude Ranch.

"Dr. Les!" Andy Parker stepped out and yelled from the tack room. "She's had one so far but something might be wrong."

"Hey there, Les. Sorry to get you out in the middle of a stormy night." Jesse Brandon reached toward his friend and neighboring ranch hand.

Les shook his hand. "Think nothing of it, Jesse. I wouldn't know how to help these mamas out if it was a decent hour of day." Both men laughed.

Les Kane worked as ranch foreman for the Double OO, a few miles up the road. Once it leaked out that he was a licensed veterinarian, the local ranches kept him busier than what he had time for. But his boss and owner of the Double OO, Judd Luke, gave him all the time he needed to help out their neighbors.

Tonight, Jesse's twelve year old collie, Pup, was having a hard time with her *late in life* surprise. His stepson, Andy Parker, had called him claiming his dad might be real hurt if Pup didn't get help. Les, along with the rest of the ranch crew had a soft spot for Andy. For an eight year old, he had a grown-up way of trying to take care of the people and animals around him.

Les squatted down beside Pup. She whined and beat her tail up and down on the concrete floor in welcome, but after examining her, he realized she was definitely in a little trouble. "It's okay, little mamma. You've got a great big baby up there."

Les glanced up at Jesse. "Probably what we call uterine inertia. She can't contract and push the baby on through. Her age is probably a big factor. Let's hope it's the last pup in there."

Twenty minutes later, Les pulled the pup free of the birth canal. It was twice the size of the first one and wasn't breathing. He worked hard to get a response from it, but it didn't happen. Pup seemed to be all right and her one baby girl was already sucking some lunch before he headed back to his cabin at the Double OO.

The rain storm had let up by the time Les pulled up to his secluded log cabin. It had been used in earlier times by city friends of Judd Luke's as a weekend getaway. But it was staying vacant too often these days. Les was asked to move into it from the bunk house a few months ago to help keep it in better condition. He was given the foreman's job a year and a half ago after Doyle Williamson had moved somewhere else. Doyle had taken a liking to Les and taught him the old cowboy way. Said he was a natural.

He pulled off his boots, slicker and hat inside the front door, then immediately went for a quick shower and crawled back into the big king log bed.

He hadn't been of a mind to think about his old life in Joplin, Missouri in a while, until tonight. His head began to throb.

It was Pup that had conjured this up tonight, and Pup's dead puppy that couldn't be saved.

He really didn't want to think about this, but scenes were moving of their own volition through his mind. Images he had finally buried were raising straight up from the dead.

He saw Mae-Belle lying on her side on the cold concrete floor in the barn. He had known before he even got to her that she was already gone. But he went through the motions to try and make her breathe anyway. He saw Jason Grace collapsed on top of Mae-Belle's body. That scene used to overwhelm him, leaving despair in his soul so heavy he would go off alone and weep. He had caused the whole thing. His carelessness had killed that family's pet, but more than a pet.

He squeezed his eyes tight trying to force away what he knew was coming. But it came just the same. Kaitlyn. Her face was a storm of pain that day like he'd never seen on anyone before. Her words had sliced his heart apart. He refused to remember them now.

He had been in love with Kaitlyn Grace. He had never been in love before her, nor since. Of course, he'd been so busy the past few years keeping to himself, there was no chance for opportunity. Maybe it just took these years to heal up the worst of his heartbreak. Because now that he was really paying attention, he realized that in the wake of this memory attack, his heart beat was slow and easy. He wasn't feeling the raw heart sickness that these images usually brought with them.

He wondered about Kaitlyn. Had she found someone else? Was she married? How was her father?

Then he slept soundly.

Some people seemed to thrive on chaos and quick changes in their daily routines, and Kaitlyn figured she should be well versed in the art by now. But somehow she always managed to be surprised when it happened. Today was no exception.

18

She walked into the veterinary office and inquired about the little dog and the bill. An older, salt and pepper haired woman behind the desk nodded at her. "Wait here. I'll be right back."

And right back she was, her arms full of a beautiful young brown spotty spaniel. The pup was well groomed and sported a happy face.

"What a little darling," Kaitlyn cooed.

"Glad you think so—she's going home with you."

The announcement startled Kaitlyn, especially since she hadn't recognized the pup as the one she had hit with her car a couple weeks ago. She just stood there with big rounded eyes.

"Here you go." The woman forced the furry bundle into Kaitlyn's arms and smiled. "She's as good as new. Just needs a place to call home. Dr. Van says there's no charge. She's his pro-bono...does a freebie once a month...his way of giving back."

"But..." Her eyes were still bugged. She attempted an argument, but couldn't drum one up to save herself. She did bring the dog in here. Stands to reason she would be expected to take it back out. "Well, okay. Is there anything I need to know about his...?"

"Her."

"Her injuries."

"No. She was just knocked unconscious. Had a pretty bad concussion, but she recovered well. She's been fully vaccinated and wormed." The woman reached out to pat the dog's head. "I would have taken her home with me, but I already did that with three other mutts. I'd be divorced by noon tomorrow if I dragged another one home. She's a sweetheart, though. Not a mean bone in her." She patted the head again. "See ya, girl," then turned suddenly and disappeared through an open doorway; but not before Kaitlyn saw the tears that had welled up beneath the woman's eyeglasses.

She sucked a long breath and exhaled slowly. "Well, pooch, looks like it's me and you, babe."

Suddenly a voice shouted its way back through the door that the woman had exited. "Her name is Bonnie."

Kaitlyn glanced down into what appeared to be the face of a laughing dog; A very *smart*, laughing dog. And she fell in love.

"Okay, Miss Bonnie. I hope you like road trips!"

Way before Kaitlyn had crossed the Wyoming state line, she and Bonnie had bonded fast and hard. A girl had never been crazier about a dog nor a dog about a girl. A one-stop shopping excursion to Walmart before heading west out of Joplin, filled the front passenger bucket seat with Bonnie, atop her own fluffy, overstuffed pillow bed. The back floor carried a bucket of Kibbles and Bits and doggie treats, a leash and bottled water. Bonnie's new hot pink collar jingled with her tags from the vet's office and a not too pretty strip of plastic with Kaitlyn's name and cell number sharpied onto it just in case they got separated.

The pair spent their second night on the road in Jackson Hole at an old west style motel that welcomed canine guests.

And until she had rolled into town and recognized some of the streets and shops, Kaitlyn hadn't once thought of Jesse Brandon. But with a heart-in-her-throat jolt, she remembered.

Her mind had felt so scrambled after losing her family and then Les.

After her father's death, Lisa and Val had brainstormed a *fun* trip for the three of them to a dude ranch in cowboy-studded Wyoming. And Kaitlyn was ready to go off somewhere that she could forget it all for a few days. The three of them had laughed all the way from Missouri to Wyoming and run amuck in Jackson Hole at night after horseback riding, hiking, eating real chuck wagon grub and flirting their wiggling backsides off with the cowboys at High Point Dude Ranch. The only problem, Kaitlyn fell for Jesse Brandon on the rebound from breaking up with Les Kane. And Jesse fell for her. She knew he was in love with her. She thought she loved him. One of those *love at first sight* things— whirlwind romance right out of a typical romance novel.

Everything had happened so fast, including marriage plans, until her discovery just one week before she would have ruined not only her life, but Jesse's as well.

Her girlfriends had gone home to jobs and left her there in her pre-wedding bliss. Bliss that changed to stark reality after a home pregnancy test awakened her to the truth that she was still in love with Les Kane. He was the father of the baby she was carrying and she had to find out where he had gone.

All she remembered after that was her desperate desire to go home and to find Les. She knew she wasn't where she belonged.

-336 That was all she remembered, until she pulled into Jackson Hole last evening. Lord help, it was a two-week whirlwind romance! Two weeks! Two weeks out of all the pain and regrets of her entire life. The memory of it kept her up most of the night; thoughts spinning with the horror of what she had done three years ago to a man who probably hated her after that with more passion than he had ever loved her with.

She had run away and left Jesse almost standing at the altar. One week before they would have exchanged wedding vows on the pavilion at High Point, Jesse's dude ranch, she asked some cowboy who was out painting fences to drive her to the closest airport, then paid him cash to forget he did it.

And until now, she had forgotten what she had done. She wondered what had happened in Jesse's life after the cruel, ruthless act she had committed against him.

Was it ever going to end—this list of conscience cleaners she'd written in rehab? She pulled her red leather journal out of her purse and added Jesse Brandon's name to that list. Her insides felt cold and sharp like splintered ice. Even remembering that God was always with her, would never forsake her, didn't warm her up this time. She just had to believe He was there, that He didn't lie to her, because she felt nothing, but achingly alone.

Around noon the next day, Kaitlyn checked out of the motel with Bonnie in tow. The plan was to pay a visit to High Point and hopefully find Jesse quickly and offer her apologies.

That thought sounded so hollow after what she'd done, but that's all she knew to do about it. And she *was* sorry for what she'd done to him—shamefully remorseful. She decided if he hated her, it was her just due.

Thankfully, the motel offered Internet service. She was able to pull up a map showing directions to the Double OO where she hoped to find Les. The motel brochure rack had one for High Point. After comparing her directions for the day, she found both ranches on the same highway, a few miles apart. That could be good—or not. She just really needed to get this day over with before she canceled it altogether. Then, by bedtime tonight, she and her four legged companion would be way down the road toward home.

Before pulling out from the motel, Kaitlyn closed her eyes a minute. *Father God, thank You for ordering my steps today.*

She hadn't been driving more than a few miles along a narrow, winding two-lane when her nerves got the best of her. How on earth did Les end up practically next door to that dude ranch…to Jesse Brandon's ranch? Oh, heaven help. She wasn't ready to face this. Les Kane was one event, but adding Jesse into the mix was overwhelming.

Kaitlyn's heart started pounding almost the instant raindrops began pelting her windshield. She thought maybe she should turn around.

Bonnie seemed to catch her master's panic attack. She sat up straight, ears alert and looked at Kaitlyn and whimpered.

And that's when it happened. She had smelled rain in the air all morning, but all at once a furious gust of wind and water attacked the driver's side of the car. Kaitlyn reached a hand out to comfort Bonnie as the steering wheel suddenly jerked to the right and out of her other hand. The sudden sheet of water cascading down the car windows blocked her view and the next thing she became aware of was the front passenger door hanging wide open and Bonnie disappearing out of it. The car had slowed almost gently and then thudded to a stop.

"Bonnie! Oh, no!" She couldn't see past the open car door with the typhoon-like wind and rain coming down, but she scooted across the seat and jumped out.

"Bon...nie. Come here, girl." She couldn't hear her own voice and knew Bonnie couldn't either. Luckily, she saw and felt the barbed wire fence just inches from the open car door and managed to mash the top down enough to high step over it."

"Bon...nie," she yelled again.

She began to run after a web of lightening lit the open field in front of her. Her feet seemed to be flying. She couldn't feel the ground, but a fearless adrenaline pushed her on. She had to find Bonnie.

It was amazing how fast the weather could change in this place. The poor little pup must be terrified. Kaitlyn kept running and calling to her. The rain poured and the wind wailed and whipped her heavy drenched hair across her face. She couldn't lose this dog. Bonnie was all she had. She must be scared to death. Maybe injured.

A dark cloud rolled in and joined the wind and rain, creating a new surge of panic. But the panic was for her lost

Bonnie. She had never been able to save a single soul in her life.

Her mind whirled with old grief that seemed to blow in with each gust of the storm. Her mom had driven away without so much as a look back. Her brother died without one word of *I'll miss you.* And her dad had grieved to death over the loss of his son. She ran faster, frantic to outrun the taunting whistles in the wind. Les. Mae-Belle. Bonnie. And there was one more, but just as it came to throw the cruelest dart of all, the ground shifted under her feet, and then disappeared completely. She screamed and frantically clawed at the air. Then a body slamming thud shot pain from her right foot clear up to her head. Her whole body seemed to vibrate. Or maybe that was just the rain pounding her into the ground.

She lay still for a minute and tried to get a clear thought into her head. The sky lit again and thunder rolled. For a moment she almost forgot it was daytime. The dark cloud was black and angry.

Okay. She needed to think. Stay calm. She was alive and probably not hurt too bad. She had fallen off of a precipice of some kind. She would just have to climb back up.

She pushed herself to a sitting position, then to her knees. When she pulled her foot beneath her to stand, a shaky yelp escaped. Landing back on her rear end, her right hand automatically moved to examine the ankle and foot. After attempting to stand, it had begun to throb. Then for the first time, she felt the cold begin to penetrate her jeans and lightweight jacket.

"Ouch." She reached down and took the tennis shoe off of her injured foot. The rain had let up to a light sprinkle, but the black cloud hung low.

She looked up toward where she had fallen off the edge of the world. She couldn't believe she survived from that high. But then, she wasn't out of here yet. Her leg could be broken. It appeared she was lost in an uninhabited wilderness, unless a pack of hungry wolves or a bear came along looking for lunch. And nobody in the entire world knew she was even in the state of Wyoming.

A fresh surge of panic gave her strength to push herself up to stand. With her weight fully on her left leg, she moaned as the change in position brought a nauseating throb to her ankle.

" Lord, help." It appeared she had dropped onto a canyon ledge, too high to climb out and too far down and treacherous looking to go farther down. She was stranded and for the first time, really scared.

Her head was pounding, her ankle killing her, until she sat back down. And because she just needed to, she cried.

After indulging herself a few moments, she breathed deep and gathered up her scattered wits. She wasn't a cry baby or a quitter, even though this moment severely tested those two character traits that she was so proud of.

She thought about the prayer she had said just minutes before driving out of Jackson Hole. *Lord, thank You for ordering my steps today.* That was the prayer she had chosen in rehab as her daily request of God. Each patient had to choose a one line prayer from a list. For the first time, she wondered if she might have picked the wrong one. Either God dropped the ball on this one or His sense of humor was *not* funny!

The storm appeared to be over, the dark cloud heading for the horizon. But the bright light of day didn't improve the situation.

After a quick unprofessional exam, she didn't think her ankle was broken, but badly sprained. There was only one thing she could think of to help herself now. She leaned back against the wall of the cliff and very earnestly prayed.

***

CHAPTER TWO

Laura Brandon had delivered her and Jesse's baby daughter, Anna Leigh, almost a year ago to the day. And today she was a week overdue with Jesse Dane Jr. Standing at her kitchen sink, rinsing out a few dirty dishes, a loud burp escaped before she could hold it back.

She couldn't help but giggle when she heard the boots thudding toward the kitchen.

"Are you all right?"

"For Pete's sake, Jesse, I burped!" She laughed out loud. "That's the third time you've asked me that in the past hour."

"Yeah, I know. But the last time you were this pregnant and made a noise like that, a baby flew out of you."

She laughed harder. "Well, let's hope we get so lucky this time...Andy's birth was brutal."

Jesse stepped behind her at the sink and wrapped his long arms around her huge belly. "Just in case, I'll be here to catch him if he shoots out like his sister did. Where is Andy, by the way?"

Laura dried her hands and turned in her husband's arms to face him. She never failed to see the passionate longing in his eyes when he looked at her. This cowboy was so madly in love with her, even after going on three years of marriage. They had never gotten past the honeymoon—Lucky her.

Laura and her five year old son, Andy Parker, came here to High Point Dude Ranch for a couple of weeks' vacation after Laura's husband, who was Andy's father, Matthew Parker, was killed in a car wreck. Matt and Jesse had grown up together and fate seemed to have sent Laura and Andy far north and right into Jesse Brandon's waiting arms. But Jesse knew it was God who brought them together. And even though Laura had been raised to believe God was only a fairy tale, she knew better now.

Jesse had taken Andy to raise like his own and as a growing family, they've shared the work load, side by side, running their dude ranch and learning to let Almighty God be the center of their lives.

Jesse bent his head and kissed his wife, long and leisurely.

"You know, this is the very thing that turns into making more of these Brandon babies," Laura teased. "And to answer your question...Andy went out to check on the petting zoo animals. He was afraid the storm might have scared the baby lambs."

"Well, guess I better go out there with him—make sure everybody's all calm and bedded down." Jesse kissed the top of her head.

"You're such a good dad, Jesse. A good *zoo* daddy too."

Before Jesse could step away to leave, Andy came quietly in the back door.

"Mom? Dad?" He spoke in such a grown up voice for an eight year old. Andy had matured beyond his years it seemed. He had taken on a lot of responsibilities working with his step dad and the ranch hands. He had taken to riding and throwing a rope like he was born for it. And he seemed to prefer the adult company around him to his school friends. His mannerisms were quiet and gentle. Kind.

Jesse turned around, one arm still around Laura. "What's up, son?"

"There's a dog in the lamb pen. He's curled up in the corner, wet and scared. I think some of the wet might be blood, but I didn't try to touch him."

Jesse rolled his eyes as he headed for the back door. "Some heartless idiot probably dumped it out on the road."

"I think it has a collar on, Dad." Andy followed him out.

Dad. Jesse still reacted every time he heard that come out of his stepson's mouth. Andy was five when Jesse married his mom. The day they returned from their three day honeymoon, Andy had jumped into his arms and said "Hi, Dad. I'm your boy now." That moment went down into the history of Jesse's heart as his all-time favorite moment. The next moment was the birth of his and Laura's baby daughter, Anna Leigh. Both

30

events had him bawling like a big ole baby as soon as he got a moment alone. Of course, finding Laura, the absolute love of his life, fell into a different category of his heart all together.

As the pair approached the petting zoo, Jesse instructed Andy to stay back a few steps. It was a medium sized, half drowned, collie looking dog. Sure enough, there was some kind of collar around its neck. Jesse squatted down several feet away and tried to coax the dog to come to him first. Its' eyes were mixed with pain and fear.

"It's okay, boy. You came here for help, didn't you?" He held his hand out. "Come here. I'll help you."

The dog growled, but didn't move.

"Here, try this." Laura had brought out a bowl of canned dog food.

Jesse set it down in front of himself. "Come here and you can have this."

When the dog got up on its front legs and whined, but couldn't go any farther, he knew the pup was injured. He put the bowl down in front of the dog and she licked it clean in seconds.

"At least he's got a good appetite. That's a good sign," Andy said as he sank onto his knees beside Jesse.

"That's for sure," Jesse answered, not amazed in the least, anymore, at Andy's reasonability. "But, why don't you run to the house and call Dr. Les. Ask him if he can spare a few minutes to come check this little guy out."

"Okay." Andy jumped up and ran toward the house.

"Andy, Pup is sleeping in the office—Don't let her out. She might not take a shine to our visitor here," Jesse yelled over his shoulder.

"Okay, I won't."

Pup was Jesse's four legged best friend before Andy came along. The joke around the ranch was that Jesse had gotten a boy for his dog. Whichever way it went, one was rarely seen without the other.

Laura went inside to check on the baby. Some days her naps lasted thirty minutes, some days two hours.

Much of the time, Martha, Laura's best friend in the world, who was Jesse's housekeeper for years before Laura came to High Point, was here keeping an eye on Anna Leigh. The two women had earned themselves a reputation as mischief artists when they decided High Point Ranch needed a major facelift a few years back. Somehow, they both came out of it smelling like roses, even to the point of each acquiring a husband since then.

Martha had finally wrangled the chuck wagon cook, Hank Walton, into the dude ranch hot tub with her one star-studded midnight. Two days later, they eloped to the neighboring ranch where Judd Luke, an ordained pastor, married them. The pastor made a note to have the water checked at High Point first chance he got. Jesse and Laura Brandon had eloped over to his ranch in the exact same fashion a few years earlier.

Judd's residential ministry, better known as his in-home cowboy church, got to be a real riot at times. There were very few dull moments in God's business up in this Wyoming ranching area. And Pastor Judd, along with his wife, Toni, enjoyed every minute of it.

Hank Walton and his blushing bride, Martha, age sixty-four and fifty-three respectively, worked tirelessly for the Brandon's dude ranch operation. Hank cooked and served the chuck wagon chow. Martha took on most of the laundry and cabin and teepee cleaning. Together the pair stood in as the only claim to grandparents that the Brandon kids had.

Tonight, the two rode out the storm in their little cedar log cabin where Hank had lived before he married Martha. And he had kept real quiet about being sweet on Miss Martha until she finally proposed to him—Martha style!

She had taken years of his pretending that he wasn't attracted to her. He *was* and she could tell it. Finally, she got fed up and stomped on long, skinny legs out to the chuck wagon about midmorning just before a crowd of trail riding dudes was due back for lunch. She grabbed the big metal spoon he was lazily using to stir a cauldron of his homemade chili with, looked him straight in his pale, shocked face and spilled her guts. *"Hank Walton, I'm in love with you. I've been battin' my eyelids at you until I'm near blind and all I get back is a grin and a nod.* Splatters of red chili dotted his face and battered his old Stetson while she shook the spoon at him. *"I'm not getting any younger here and neither are you. Now one of us is gonna die alone, most likely, but there's no need in both of us having to do it alone. Do you want to marry me or not?"*

Hank stared at her for a long time until the shock of her audacity finished weaving through him. Funny how timid he had felt around women his whole life, right up until just about one minute ago. He reached up and dragged his hat off of his head then spoke without batting an eye. *"It's a fact, Miss Martha, I've been sweet on you for some time now. It's...well, I just don't have anything to offer a woman."* He moved his hand toward the chili pot. *"This right here is about all I have and a little cabin on a little bit of land. What woman would settle for that?"*

She looked at him like there was something wrong with his face. *"Was that a yes or a no?"*

He looked away, then back at her. *"Shouldn't we go on a date or something first?"*

Quick as lightening, she snapped back, *"Apple cobbler and coffee and a dip in the hot tub. Midnight. How does that sound?"*

The most beautiful mouth of straight white teeth Martha had ever seen suddenly gleamed into her face. *"Just fine. Just fine."*

The storm had finally blown itself out and left the air colder than normal. Hank and Martha Walton sat out in their porch swing, something they rarely had time for. The dude ranch had shut down for a couple of weeks to give the hands time off, and Jesse and Laura time to prepare for the birth of Jesse Jr.

Hank settled an arm around his bride of two years and enjoyed her sharp wit and humor. She never failed to make him laugh out loud. He shifted his gaze out into the darkness for a moment, but it was long enough for the odd light shining a ways off through the trees to catch his eye. At first, he thought he was imagining it, but no, there was some sort of light out there.

"Do you see a light through those trees, Hon?" He pointed in the direction.

Martha bent down a little and squinted into the darkness. "Yes, I do. Wonder what that could be. There's nothing over that way but rocks and canyons."

Hank gave her a sideways glance. "You up for a little adventure?"

"Sure. You know me. Maybe it's one of those UFO's with a creature from space…might be scary."

Hank got a flashlight out of his truck and they headed off at a brisk walk on the shoulder of the road. "Only thing scary out here is me, woman. You lead the way. I've got your back."

She laughed out loud.

A good half mile out, they came up on a small car with Missouri plates. The interior dome light was burning, the front passenger door wide open. The car was sitting cockeyed off in the ditch and stuck deep in mud.

Martha looked inside and saw a woman's coin purse on the floorboard. "The keys are in the ignition, Hank. Something seems real wrong about this." She glanced in the back floor board. "Whoever this belongs to has a dog. Its food is in the back."

Hank had been scouting around the outside with his flashlight. He held up a soaked piece of padded material that was half buried in the mud beside the opened front door. "This looks like a dog bed like Pup sleeps on in the ranch office." He laid it back down.

Martha cupped her hands around her mouth and called out. "Hello. Anybody out there?"

It was deathly quiet. They listened a minute, then she called again.

Nothing.

Then a tiny strangled crying sound came through the blackness.

They shot a look at each other, and then Martha called out again.

Nothing.

"Hank, something is wrong here. I feel it. Let's cross the fence and walk out a piece."

He started to move toward the fence, but stopped when he realized that anything could be out there and he wasn't going to risk getting Martha hurt, either by something or someone. The woman was too gung ho for her own good. And he told her so.

"Let's get back to the house and call Jesse," Hank reasoned. "Might ought to get more help in case somebody *is* out there."

They got back to the cabin to find the phone line was dead. "Storm must have got it," Hank said. "Get in the truck—We'll drive over."

Hank was fairly certain no one would have crossed that fence rather than walking up the road to find help, unless somebody was up to no good. But that small squeaking sound in the air couldn't be ignored.

Martha hadn't said a word all the way back to the cabin. Hank didn't think she had ever been this quiet, this long, since he'd married her. Halfway to High Point, Martha's silence finally got to him.

"Why are you so quiet, Hon?"

When she didn't answer, he reached for her hand. She had just wiped her cheek and her fingers were wet.

Without another word, Hank pulled the truck to the shoulder of the road, stopped and threw it in park. He had never seen this woman cry. Not once. And it shook him to his core.

He reached for her, but she tried to wave him off. Normally, he would have left her alone if she said to. But, he caught both of her upper arms and forced her around to face him.

"Martha, you'd best be telling me why you're crying, because until you do, this truck's not moving one inch." He held her in place.

"Oh lord, Hank. I can't say it. You'd just tell me what a silly old woman I am."

He looked her sternly in the eye. "Try me. I've never known you to be at a loss for words, young lady. And I've never seen a tear in your eyes before neither. Tell me what I did."

"I feel like a fool now. It's just that you made it clear we couldn't cross that fence because you were worried about my safety. I never knew what it felt like until now to have somebody say that they cared about me in that way. You put *me* ahead of *everything.*"

Hank looked stricken. "Are you telling me that I've never told you how much you mean to me? Have I never said it?"

"Not like that—But I'm just being silly. I know I am."

"No, you're not." Hank pulled his wife into his arms and wrapped her thin, taut body tightly against him. He held her with such strength, she began to cry again.

"I'm the fool here—not you. Martha, the past couple of years have been the only ones in my whole life that count for me. I can't take a chance on something happening to you. There'd be nothing left for me without you. I've tried to show you that. I mean, I get that we're what's called the old folks around here, but we rocked that old cabin off its cement blocks many times. Guess I could throw in a few more words now and then to go with it."

Martha burst out laughing. Hank joined her.

After a minute, he caught her face between his hands and kissed her deeply. "We almost went our whole lives and never experienced being in love," Hank said, after he finally let her get some air. "Like you said, we could have both died alone and never..." He grinned like a cat with a mouse. "Bet this old truck could rock..."

"Hank?"

"Yeah?"

"One of us is going to die *tonight* if this truck's not going down the road in ten seconds. And *I* ain't dyin."

He rose up straight and got back behind the wheel. "Gotcha."

Then, Martha scooted over and snuggled close against him.

Jesse and Andy were standing in the lamb pen when Dr. Les Kane pulled into the yard and parked beside the petting zoo entrance. He stepped out of his truck and strode quickly to Jesse's side, offering his hand.

"Evening, Jesse...Andy."

"Hey there, Les. Thanks for coming over. I promise you, I'll try to need a vet on a nice sunny day next time."

Les laughed. "No problem, man." He popped Jesse on the shoulder then spied the little wet dog sitting on his haunches in the corner of the pen giving off fearful and warning looks. "Who's the newcomer?"

"Don't know. Andy found him out here, but he won't come to us—Looks like he might be hurt in his back end."

-336 "Yeah, and I think he has a collar on, too." Andy offered.

"At first," Jesse said, "I thought somebody dumped him, but probably not with a collar on."

Les walked up to the shivering dog and reached his hand out to let him smell him. At first, the dog's eyes grew large and fearful, and then he sniffed the back of Les's hand and licked at it. Les squatted down and gently rubbed the long nose with his knuckles. "Good boy. I'm not going to hurt you." He rubbed his hand down the dog's neck, then down his side. A tiny whimper came from the pup as he touched close to the hindquarters. "Take it easy." Les's voice was barely above a whisper. "Let's see what you're wearing here." He unbuckled the collar and shoved it into his jacket pocket. "Okay, let's get you on all four legs. I know you can do it—You got here on them." He helped the whimpering dog stand, and then quickly examined his hips and back legs before he let him sit again.

He walked back to where Jesse waited with Andy by the fence. "First off, our good boy over there is a girl. I think she's just bruised—Could have been hit by a car or..."

Headlights bounced up the drive causing all three to turn around and look.

"That's Cook or Martha or both," Jesse said.

Hank, known simply as Cook around the ranch, and Martha joined the group and exchanged greetings.

"We come by tonight because we thought somebody could be in need of some help."

"What's going on, Hank?" Jesse turned fully towards him declaring his undivided attention to the older gentleman.

Hank and Martha in turn related their story.

Les had taken a mini-flashlight out of his pocket and while listening to the Walton's story, he examined the dog collar. A small plastic tube was taped to the collar. When he finally pulled all the tape off, he discovered a laminated, oblong strip of pink paper inside. Holding the light on it, he read, *Hi, I'm Bonnie. If you find me, call Kaitlyn.* A cell phone number ended the note.

Les lifted his head to find several pairs of eyes trained on him.

"Les, you look a little shocked. You all right?" Jesse glanced at the stuff in Les's hands, then back at his face.

"Yeah, Jesse, I'm good. Hank, did you say that car had Missouri tags?"

"Yes, it did." Martha answered the question. "And a woman's small coin purse and Hank found a dog bed like pup's outside the door in the mud. But we thought we might have heard a noise out in the dark, kinda way off. Could have been a coyote, but we..."

Les was already heading for his truck. "Bring whatever flashlights you have."

It took a stunned few seconds before everybody moved. Jesse sent Andy in to tell Laura the story and he jumped in with Les.

"Stop at my truck over there, Les, so I can get a flashlight."

After they were on their way, Jesse couldn't help but see the panic on Les's face. "Is there something you know about this? Were you expecting a visitor or...?"

Les was shaking his head. His emotions were in a riot. Could that be Kaitlyn Grace? What would she be doing way up here?

Jesse picked up the dog collar and note off of the seat where Les had thrown it. He held up the pink strip and shined his flashlight on it. "Well, this doesn't leave much to wonder about. Our friend is Bonnie and belongs to Kaitlyn." Les seemed to be in a mood, so he didn't say anymore.

In a few minutes, Les pulled onto the shoulder of the road and joined his headlights with Hanks to light up the abandoned black, late model Toyota and the area around it.

Hank pulled the keys from the ignition and opened the trunk. A suitcase, jacket, boots. No purse. The coin purse in the floor of the car contained a few dollars and change. No identification. Les pulled the suitcase up on top of the other stuff in the truck and unzipped it. Jeans, T's, undies. Still no purse or ID. She must have taken it with her.

Jesse came around back and handed Les a card. It was an auto insurance card he found in the glove box. "Kaitlyn Grace," Jesse quoted. "Does that name mean anything to you?"

Les grabbed the card and looked at it. "I know her. But I wasn't expecting her here for any reason."

The two men's faces jerked toward the darkness of the open range and canyons across the fence as they heard Martha's loud, throaty yell. "Hel...lo. Can you hear me?"

They all barely breathed as they strained to hear sounds, but it was deathly quiet.

Les didn't know what would be worse for her—to be out here in the dark somewhere or picked up by someone in a vehicle. A wrong someone. Damn it! He headed toward the fence as he scanned as far out as the beam from his flashlight would go. "Kaitlyn!"

Again they all strained to hear, but nothing.

Les stepped over the fence and the rest followed. They spread out a few yards apart, Hank having to work to keep step with his wife.

Had minutes passed? Hours? When Kaitlyn opened her eyes, she was curled in a fetal position with her head resting on a flat rock about the size of a dinner plate and she was freezing. Her clothes were very wet and clung to her skin. The only word she could come up with was *yuck!*

The last thing she remembered was leaning against the cliff wall and telling God she was all His. She wasn't so sure He had heard her prayer. Probably wasn't looking when she went over the cliff and had no idea where she went.

She sat up and tried to adjust her eyes to the darkness. There was no moon or stars. Just black clouds letting the darkness swallow her up. Figured!

She realized suddenly what woke her up. She had been dreaming that Les Kane had called her name. The sound of his voice was still shouting in her head. The sound of her name on his lips rolled back the layers of years that had safely kept her feelings for him in a tidy little box. Her dream, the sound of his voice, had just shattered that box.

She suddenly yearned to see Les's face, to hear his voice. That feeling scared her because she didn't come here to start up with Les again. He could be in love with someone else. Or married. He deserved to have his life all together and happy. She wished that for him, especially after the horrible way she had hurt him.

A sob hiccupped out of her mouth before she even knew she was crying. A light drizzle began to fall and she lay back down and hid her face in the crook of her arm. *I sowed pain and destruction in Les Kane's heart. Now I was sent up here to reap it back. I deserve to die right here.* Kaitlyn's insides felt as black as the velvet rain falling on top of her.

"Kait...lyn!"

Without thinking, she jerked herself upright and jumped to her feet, forgetting her ankle. She hadn't felt the pain until she jumped up on it at the sound of her name out in space somewhere. She yelped at the stab that went through her foot and ankle.

That was no dream. "Down here! I'm down here!" She stood motionless and listened. There was no sound. "Here. I'm here," she tried again. She listened hard, almost sure she could hear people talking. But they sounded so far away.

Her ankle had begun to throb until she flopped back down on her rear and massaged her leg. That only seemed to make it hurt worse.

"Hello." She yelled as loud as she could around the lump in her throat. "I'm here, somebody." She could barely hear her own voice now. "I'm here." She let her voice trail off in a hopeless little whisper. "God, send some help for me." She barely moved her lips as she prayed and she couldn't hear her own voice at all.

She decided her mind had been playing tricks on her with the voices. It was still sprinkling rain. Even the weather had something against her.

She curled up on the cold, wet, rocky ground, desperately wanting to sleep. She was shivering cold and the rocky surface underneath bit into her head and shoulder and hip. She could tell her foot and ankle had swelled somewhat and the pain was almost unbearable.

As a child, when things got too emotionally painful to cope, Kaitlyn learned to fantasize her way through it. The moment that memory came into her mind, she imagined Les's body spooned around her, his long arm draped over her, holding her close and warm. Her throbbing foot forgotten, the chill assuaged, she drifted into a fitful sleep. When consciousness tried to break through, she pushed herself tighter into Les's curled body and slept on.

Bonnie is barking, she thought indistinctly. She's so loud! The barking went on and on. She wanted to wake up enough to go quiet her down, but she couldn't seem to get there. Les could make her be quiet. But she didn't want him to get up and leave her. But he did anyway. She felt the full blast of cold again as his fingers caught her arms and forced her onto her back.

"Les," she cried out. "Don't leave. Les."

"Kaitlyn, I'm here. Open your eyes."

Blinking and fighting to get above the intense drowsiness, she tried to push herself to sit up, but two hands held her down.

Finally, her focus cleared. "Les?" she whispered. She felt like crying with relief.

Her gaze found the face of the man she was fantasizing about, imagining he was holding her. But this was no fantasy. Les was kneeling beside her, leaning over her, holding her flat to the ground, his wide brown eyes boring into hers. Lightening shot through the darkness and Kaitlyn caught a clear glimpse of fear on his face. Or was it anger?

"My God, Kaitlyn. What are you doing out here?"

She couldn't blurt out the answer to that question. His eyes were ablaze with an angry confusion now and she really wanted to get up off of her back. "I can get up. Just my ankle is hurt."

A clap of thunder suddenly shot through the canyon so loud, Kaitlyn screamed and covered her face with her hands. The downpour came—the one to end all downpours.

Les pulled her hands from her face and helped her to sit up. "Are you sure you're not hurt anywhere besides your ankle?" He had to yell to be heard over the pounding rain.

She nodded in response. Les stood and pulled her up onto her feet at the same time, then looked up and yelled a deep, booming, "Jesse!" toward the top of the ridge.

"Right here!" shot back at them.

"We're pulling her up. Get ready."

Les picked up a rope with a loop that he'd lowered himself down on. The other end was wrapped around a large rock projection up top. He put the loop over her head and secured it under her arms.

"Kaitlyn, this is probably going to be a little painful. Grit your teeth and help all you can with your good foot. We've got to get you out of here. There are people up on the top of the ridge ready to pull you up. Ready?"

She nodded and braced her uninjured foot against the wall. Out of this entire ordeal, all she could do was dread to pop up over the top of this canyon and find herself face to face with Jesse Brandon—Not the way she had planned this little mission trip.

And neither had she planned on the reaction her entire being took on at the sight of Les on his knees beside her and the jolt her heart suffered at the touch of his hands when he held her to the ground. Of course, she might have reacted the same way if some half-wit mountain man had jumped down to rescue her from this wet, freezing tomb. But she doubted that.

Kaitlyn had not just loved Les Kane. She was *in love* with Les Kane. And that never went away. She'd had to force her thoughts away from him in order to get through her days and nights since she had driven him away.

He looked different than she remembered—thinner, older. His fingers felt like an iron vise when they gripped her arms. But it was the hard lines etched into his sun browned face that stood out the most. She almost wished that telling blaze of lightening hadn't shown him up so clearly. A fresh crack splintered across her heart.

She felt a tug on the rope and a stern, "Grab that rope and *do not* let go."

That's the last thing she remembered about the trip out of her outdoor prison. She was suddenly sitting on solid ground with several pairs of hands assisting her at once.

A woman's face appeared right in front of her, somebody's grandmother who took Kaitlyn's hands in hers and rubbed them. A man-sized coat was draped over her head and the lady reached and pulled it tight around Kaitlyn's small drenched frame.

Small beams of light flittered beside her, then away. It finally registered that her rescuers had flashlights. The wet cold had penetrated through her to the bone, her ankle was throbbing wildly and she was consumed with shame. Although she was well aware that Jesse Brandon was one of the people moving around her and Les Kane was obviously a friend or close neighbor of his, Kaitlyn felt sort of disassociated from the goings on around her—a protective mechanism in the brain when emotions were too far over the top, maybe.

The rain was pounding so hard she couldn't hear any talking, just saw a lot of shadowy movement outside of her coat tent.

But it was the wet, smelly fur ball that attacked her lap and flopped over on its back and licked her face and neck and arms until she momentarily forgot about everything except Bonnie.

She didn't notice when the coat fell off of her head. She was fully involved in the moment with her lost best friend until lightening crackled too close for comfort and a pair of arms simultaneously scooped her up and took off with her at a very fast pace.

She knew it was Les and she wrapped her arms around his neck and he tightened his grip around her, pulling her closer into him. The sudden movement of her body had made her head swim. She felt like a limp noodle and for some odd reason, she felt only partly aware of her body being carried away.

After Les deposited her into the back seat of his crew cab dually, he slid in beside her and shut the door. He gently grasped her head with both hands and turned her face up where he could study it.

"Kaitlyn, tell me how you're feeling."

"I...t-told you. Just my ankle is sprained. I'm okay. Just c-cold." She could hear her own teeth clicking together. "Where's Bonnie?"

He quickly counted her pulse, and then studied her eyes. "Okay, sit still for a minute. Oh, by the way, do you have a purse somewhere?"

She nodded. "Under...m-my driver's seat."

Les got out and ran back to retrieve Kaitlyn's suitcase from the trunk of her car and grab her purse and anything else within reach before locking it up."

Jesse had headed Hank and Martha home along with the dog, at Martha's insistence. He deduced that this young lady was someone Les knew well and he probably needed to ride with her. After he slid the water out of his eyes and off of his face, he got behind the wheel and cranked up the heater. He turned his gaze toward the back seat, seeing Kaitlyn's face for the first time. She met his look and watched him recognize her. His eyes saucered, his lips dropped apart and he sat twisted around, staring, frozen. Stunned disbelief coated his whole head. He didn't say a word, but managed to break through his shock enough to turn back around and face the front when Les opened the door and slid back in beside—Katie?

"Head home, Jesse. I'll take care of everything from there," Les said.

Just then, Jesse remembered Laura. He turned on the interior light and glanced at his watch. He realized it had been three hours since he'd left his way overdue pregnant wife alone. His wife—who could slide a baby out of herself with a sneeze, for crying out loud!

Les caught on as soon as Jesse peeled out, slinging mud up on the windows. It was a short, fast ride back to the ranch.

***

CHAPTER THREE

Kaitlyn didn't ask any questions, but did as she was told and got up into the front passenger seat of the dually as soon as it screeched to a stop beside a house. With the motor and heater running and a command to "sit tight," Les went inside the back door of the house where Jesse had hurriedly disappeared a few moments ahead of him.

How could every single thing go so wrong on this trip? Kaitlyn leaned her head back feeling like the lowest of life on earth. There was no doubt that Jesse was still angry and despised the sight of her the way he tore off in the truck and then jumped out and practically ran inside, she assumed, his house. It was dark, but she didn't recognize what little she could see out of the truck window. She was sure Les was getting an earful in there about her. Maybe she should get out and go try to explain all this mess. But she felt too exhausted and disoriented to form a decent explanation. So she waited.

Les stood in the kitchen and waited for Jesse to check on Laura, to make sure his help wasn't needed. He had never helped birth a baby person before, but in a pinch, he figured he could wing it. Hopefully that would never happen to him.

But then, you never know what might happen at any minute. He had just found a woman who had slipped off of a steep embankment, out in the middle of a Wyoming canyon, wet, freezing, scared and a thousand miles from home—a woman he had almost married several years ago—a woman who had killed his pride and shredded his heart. He had spent those years hiding out on the back side of the Double OO Ranch, nursing his wounds from the back side of a horse or with a branding iron in his fist. And his *cowboying* years had served him well. The seasons came and went and he had been content to ride and rope and enjoy a little camaraderie within the ranching communities. And heal.

And now this! One stormy night and suddenly he's looking into the face that had caused him so much pain. He could hardly believe it was her. Nor could he believe the overwhelming desire that nearly cut off his air when he saw her.

For an instant, he was back on the Grace Ranch in Missouri, in love with the most beautiful woman he'd ever laid eyes on, loving, kind, sensitive Kaitlyn Grace, who had experienced more than her share of emotional trauma. It had been love at first sight for both of them. Kaitlyn had given her body to him, along with her heart. He'd been her first lover.

At that remembrance, he collected his thoughts and packed them back up. It had been a long time. And no matter what on earth she was doing out on that canyon ledge in a thunderstorm, it couldn't have a thing to do with him.

Jesse returned to the kitchen in his sock feet. "Everybody's asleep." He stared at Les a moment, questions running over each other in his head. "That girl out there, Les. Is she a friend of yours? Or family?"

"Neither." Les fidgeted and pulled on his hat brim. "I knew her a long time ago. I'll see she has a place to stay tonight and take care of her car tomorrow as soon as this storm passes."

Jesse nodded and bit his tongue to stop more questions from shooting out. He was rattled, to say the least, when he saw Katie's face in the back seat of the truck. But her name is not Kaitlyn Grace. It's Katie Lynn. Or is it?

Jesse was six days away from saying "I Do" to Katie Lynn...or whoever she is, several years ago. She had come with a couple of girlfriends to his dude ranch looking for a good time with a cowboy. Of course, he was the lucky wrangler that thought he was in love for life. But she up and left without so much as an adios. He thought his heart was beyond repair for a long time. But Laura came along and he realized that he had never been in love with Katie or anyone else, for that matter. In lust, maybe, but certainly not love. Katie had done him the greatest favor of his life by running away. It just took the right woman to come along for him to figure that out. Laura was truly the love of his life. He felt nothing but gratefulness to Almighty God at the way his life turned out and just a little confused about who Katie really is and why she was out in the middle of nowhere like that. But thankfully, she was Les's problem tonight, by his own enlistment.

"Well...holler if you need me, Jesse. Goodnight." Les went out the back door and walked to the truck, oblivious to the rain that added more wet to his already muddy and drenched frame.

He sat behind the steering wheel letting the blowing heat remind him of how cold he actually was while he sized up Kaitlyn's alertness.

"How are you feeling? Dizzy? Weak?"

She looked at him with a clear, but traumatized expression. "Just...cold...To the bone...And so dirty." Her face crinkled suddenly and she slapped a hand over her mouth, but the choking sobs came.

Les threw it in gear and headed for the Double OO. Within fifteen minutes, they were pulling up in front of his small, but rather fancy styled log house. Without a word, he got out and went around, opening her door. It was raining harder now.

Very carefully, he grasped her around her back and slid his other arm under her legs and lifted her off the truck seat as easy as he would have a small child. He carried her beneath the cover of the porch roof, and then gently lowered her feet. "Stand on your good foot—Keep the other one up," he coached her.

When he shoved open the heavy door, he reached just inside where a flip of a switch lit up several lamps around the interior. He looked down then into the depths of her ocean greens, then tightened his hold around her shoulders. "Whoa there...Hang on." He spoke softly.

She didn't realize she was light headed and off balance until Les's arm suddenly righted her. He held her steady, studying her face for signs of deepening shock. Even through the streaks of mud on her face, her dark blonde curly hair plastered against her head and stringing in all directions, his heart hammered wildly at the sight of her. Memories of the past rushed up to torment his heating flesh. He had made love with this woman twice and both times were burned into his soul like a permanent tattoo. It had been so much more than just sex. The emotional bonding that had sealed them together years ago was still there as strong as ever. At least for him!

Les had given Kaitlyn an engagement ring and their love was sealed that same night when she gave him her virgin body. Nothing could have prepared him for the devastating breach in the deepest part of his soul as the feel of his ring popping his face when she had thrown it at him and sent him away.

Suddenly, he swept her up in his arms and headed across the den and down a hallway to the bathroom. He kicked the potty lid shut with his foot and sat her down on it. He reached into the rock and tiled shower and turned on a hard spray before dropping to his knees in front of her.

"Let's get you in the shower." He removed her slip on tennis shoes and gently examined the swollen ankle and foot. "It's not broken, I'm fairly certain, but we'll see what it looks like tomorrow."

Eyes wide, Kaitlyn pushed at his hands when he reached to pull up her T-shirt. "What are you doing?" Nothing felt more natural to him than to help her out of her clothes and into the shower. "I'm not having you pass out in here and gain another injury," he said matter of fact, just before he whipped the shirt over her head. "And if you sit here much longer, I'll have a case of pneumonia on my hands."

Panic flared in her eyes as she covered her wet bra with her arms. "No, Les...You can't take off my clothes!"

"It wouldn't be the first time," he said sarcastically. He reached behind him and jerked a large bath towel off of the towel rack. "Here—Cover with this, then." There was no mistaking the edge of anger in his voice.

Inside of a minute, he had every thread she had on in a wet muddy pile and without hesitation; he pulled her up onto her feet and held her while she hobbled into the steaming shower. He pulled the towel from around her just as she stepped beneath the hard and very warm spray of water. Thankfully, the glass panes were heavily fogged over, but Les was forgotten as quickly as it took the hot water to hit the top of her head and cascade down her near frozen skin.

Les had to force his eyes away from the shower glass. He stood at the steamed-over door, catching her solid movements out of the corner of his eye. The sooner he got her out and tucked under warm covers, the better he would feel about the situation. He really wanted to know what she was doing here, but that conversation was going to have to wait at least until tomorrow.

After a couple of minutes, he pulled the door open and reached to turn off the water and thrust a towel at her.

"Here—dry off, wrap up and get out of there."

She complied without a word and when she stepped out of the stall, the towel wrapped tightly around her middle and curly, wet hair jumbled just past her shoulders, Les felt almost overwhelmed by the resurgence of feelings he had spent years trying to lose. After years of only horses, bawling calves and macho cowboys for company, by his own settlement, all of his hard won contentment to be alone seemed to have dissolved, along with the steam from the shower. He stood frozen for several seconds, clearly not prepared for the strength of his power packed emotions.

This he hadn't expected. But then, he hadn't had enough time to expect anything. Half a dozen emotions attacked all at once. He was bewildered, then agitated—dumbfounded. But mostly just plain ticked off!

One thing he knew for sure. This incident, no matter what *this* ended up being, was not going to change anything. He had learned the hard way how a woman could twist up a man's insides and he had spent years working to get his un-wadded. That was plenty for his one lifetime.

Exhaustion fell on Kaitlyn like a heavy wet blanket after stepping out of the hot shower. When her knees weakened, Les lifted her in his arms and carried her to his bedroom. He sat her on the edge of his unmade king sized log bed, leaving her long enough to pull one of his T-shirts out of a dresser drawer. Wordlessly, he dropped it over her head and pulled it down before unwrapping the damp towel from around her. Next he grabbed a pair of thick white socks from the same drawer, knelt down and worked them on her feet, then stood up. She looked up at him through half closed lids and feebly attempted a smile.

"Sit still. I'm going to warm you some soup I have left over. Be right back."

He was back inside of two minutes to discover her curled in a fetal ball, sound asleep. He set the mug of soup on the lamp table and pulled the top sheet, quilt and comforter up and tucked it all around her.

Les stood over her and stared at the small lump in his bed. She could pass for a child curled up like that. He touched her forehead, and then satisfied she didn't have a fever, stood up straight, but found he was unable to move his eyes from the side view of her face. Her lashes were dark brown lying against her pale cheek. He swallowed hard, his fists curling in his male need to protect this young defenseless little female. He just wasn't sure what or who he was doing battle with. He didn't know why she was here or why she was hurt. But standing there seeing her this way, he did get that his life had just rounded a bend—one he never saw coming until his heart flipped and made the turn. And he didn't like it one bit.

He turned and headed for the doorway, pushed down the light switch and went into the bathroom without a glance back.

In five minutes, he emerged from the shower. His towel dried hair was standing on end as he scooped up two sets of muddy clothes. He rinsed out each article of clothing in the oversized stainless sink in the laundry room just off of the kitchen, then dropped them all into the washer, doused the load with detergent and turned it on.

Almost forgetting the fact that he was *jay birding* with a house guest down the hall, he grabbed up clean folded underwear and charcoal gray sweat pants off the top of the clothes dryer and stepped into them.

Suddenly, his thirty-eight years felt more like fifty. Exhaustion of a strange sort made his arms and legs heavy and all he could think about at that moment was sleep. He'd had little rest in the past forty-eight hours, but that was normal for his work load as Double OO foreman. He was used to it. Maybe it was just catching up with him.

Les left a night light plugged in over the kitchen counter and switched the string of lamps off in the den before stretching his spent body out on the couch. Within seconds, he was asleep, but not before his mind recalled Kaitlyn's muttered words when he'd found her asleep on the canyon ledge. *Les don't leave.*

Kaitlyn opened her eyes. It was pitch dark and quiet, except for her full bladder that was yelling at her. She stared hard and blinked into the blackness, trying to recall where she was. When her eyes adjusted better, she reached for the bedside lamp that was in silhouette beside her head. She couldn't remember why she was in this strange bed, until she sat up and threw off the bed covers. When she swung her feet to the floor, the pain in her slightly larger right foot brought everything back in a hurry.

"Oww…wee," she groaned at the sharp stab in her ankle. As she reached to rub the smarting foot, she found herself in somebody's socks. She looked down at her chest. And somebody's T-shirt. And nothing else! At least the shirt fell to knee-length on her when she stood up.

Les. He must have put these clothes on her. Obviously, *his* clothes, but for the life of her, she couldn't raise a memory of it. She glanced at the digital alarm clock next to the lamp. 3:33 AM. She stood and stepped gingerly on her sore foot toward the doorway and crippled a bee line down the hall to find a potty.

Afterward, she entered the kitchen by the glow of a night light. She glanced into the den and spied Les's long bodied form curled on the couch. All he had on was a pair of dark colored sweat pants. He was bare foot and bare chested. But something didn't look right about him. She hobbled closer. No pillow. No cover. And he was shivering. More like shaking hard.

She hesitated only a moment before moving closer and touched his forehead. The shaking was fever chills. His head was burning hot.

Suddenly Les bolted off of the couch and grabbed Kaitlyn by her T-shirt front. Her sharp scream was all that kept him from throwing a punch at her. His racing heartbeat matched the one he could literally feel pounding the back of his fist that was twisted tightly in her shirt. He let her go.

"Damn it, Kaitlyn! I could have hurt you—sneaking up on me like that." Les felt his head swoon and he dropped back down to sit on the couch.

0   After sucking in a good breath, she found enough strength to speak. "I saw you shaking—you feel hot."

He raised his eyes up to meet hers. "I'll be fine." His voice was as rough as gravel. "Just let me sleep." His eyes dropped to her feet. "How's the foot?"

She wasn't even aware that she had a foot right then. She was only aware of a warm desire to reach out and smooth back his rumpled hair.

Finally, she stuttered a reply. "I...it...it's better."

Les looked back up and started to say something, but leaned back on the couch instead and moaned.

Kaitlyn shot a look of sympathy at him just as a surge of motherly-like *take charge* assaulted her senses. This man needed someone to take care of him right now and by all indications, she was it.

"Les, come with me." She took his hand and pulled. "You need to get in bed where you can rest better."

He pulled his hand free and lay over on the couch. "I'm *in* bed. I'll be fine." Truth was, he was so sick, he didn't think he could stand up.

"No!" She reached for his hand again and pulled, urging him to sit back up. "You are *not* in bed nor are you fine. You're sick." She pulled on his hand again. "Don't make this hard for me, Les. Come on—you're going to get in your bed."

A moan growled out of him as he forced his long, lanky frame back upright. "Lord amighty. Feels like I was rode hard and put up wet." He let her help him up to stand, but when the warm skin of her arm wrapped around his back and her fingers clutched the taut bare muscles in his side, he didn't think he could ever feel bad enough to not react to that. A shudder shot through his whole body and she gripped him tighter, mistaking the reason for it.

"Well...I'm sure you got the *wet* part right," she replied.

Les allowed her to help him to the bedroom and without preamble, he fell into the bed with a thud. If it meant saving his life, he doubted he could even raise his head up again. Nausea threatened him if he dared to move.

Kaitlyn headed for the bathroom, hobbling with a new awareness of her sprained foot. It had begun to throb again or maybe she was just now paying attention. She found pain medicine in the cabinet above the sink and took that, along with a paper cup of water and a cool wet wash rag.

"Les, I want you to raise up enough to swallow a couple of pills."

When he didn't move, she put a hand behind his too warm neck. "Raise up and take this. Come on, help me out here."

Finally, he swallowed some water and the tablets and dropped his head back down with a growling groan.

"Don't move me, Katie. I'll puke," he slurred as if it hurt to talk. Then suddenly, he began to shake with chills again. He felt a cold cloth on his forehead and knew she was trying to take care of him. He should be taking care of *her*. Her foot was hurt. But he just couldn't get there from here.

Nothing about this day made sense to Les. He wanted to be angry—to shove a slice of his years of bitterness down her throat. And he wanted to ask her half a dozen questions. He wanted her to have never come here. And he wanted to reach out and pull her into his arms and beg her not to ever leave him. But he was too sick to move a muscle or think about it anymore.

Kaitlyn sat beside him on the bed until she knew he was asleep. After one more trip to re-wet the washcloth and straighten the covers around him, she grabbed an extra pillow off the bed, along with a quilt from the closet and retreated to the couch in the den. She popped a couple of pain pills when she gave Les his and the pain in her foot was already subsiding. It didn't take her long to fall asleep.

It was loud daylight when Kaitlyn managed to open her eyes. They didn't want to open, but something jarred at them until she relented.

The front door was open letting the bright light of day in. And somebody was hammering on the door or wall.

"Hello...Les?" A deep male voice boomed inside of the hammering.

Finally, Kaitlyn raised her head and realized a big cowboy-hatted figure was making the racket.

"Hello?" Her sleep induced voice growled cautiously up at him.

"Oh. Pardon me, mam. I was looking for Les. He didn't show up at the barn this morning so...I thought..." The man's eyes darted past her toward the hallway, then back again.

She managed to get her legs over the edge of the couch and sit up before his words registered. "Oh, Les. He was sick last night which was actually the wee hours of this morning. "Fever. He was..."

Before she could get her words to come out making sense, the man strode past her and down the hall. She followed him at a hobble, her ankle not quite as ouchy this morning.

Les was buried under the bed covers in a deep sleep. Kaitlyn hurried past the cowboy and felt of Les's forehead and arm. He was still too warm, but nothing like last night.

She motioned the man to follow her as she gimped into the kitchen to find a coffee pot. She hadn't thought far enough ahead to realize she was next to naked in one of Les's T-shirts until the man handed her a white terry bath robe that had suddenly appeared in his hands. Evidently he knew his way around Les's house.

She put it on and tied the sash, then reached a hand toward him. "I'm Kaitlyn Grace."

He removed his hat and gently shook her hand. "Judd Luke." He eyed her curiously, but his eyes were kind—the type of *kind* that would draw a person to tell their life story to. "What's wrong with Les?"

"He got sick suddenly last night—chills and fever, I guess, from being wet and cold for several hours."

Then she related the story of how she managed to be lost on a cliff ledge and Les had found her—at least, as much as she could recall with any intelligence.

He looked down at her foot. "Do you want to let a doctor check out that ankle? I have a good doctor friend in Jackson Hole."

She wiggled it. "I don't think so. It's a lot better this morning. Les might be another story, though. He's still feverish."

Judd looked at her for a moment seeming to be in sudden deep thought, then turned and strode back to Les's bedroom.

"Les." He bent over and shook Les's shoulder.

"Yeah." The answer came with a growl.

"If you'll get up and get in my truck, we'll go see Doc Raye." When no answer came, he shook his shoulder again. "What do you think, cowboy?"

"Na. Can't. Be...ok...tomor..." Les felt too sick to talk, much less to get up and go somewhere.

Then Judd rested his hand on Les's shoulder and prayed. *"Lord Jesus, take care of this stubborn kid of Yours here until I can get him a doctor. Thanks. Amen."* When he turned suddenly to leave, Kaitlyn was standing in the doorway watching him. There was just something humbling about seeing a big brawny cowboy pray.

"Mam, if you..."

"It's Kaitlyn."

"Alright, Kaitlyn, if you would look after Les for a while longer, I'll get a doctor friend of mine to come out here. He might already be in the area today."

"Of course I will."

"You said Jesse Brandon helped with your rescue last night?"

She nodded.

"I'll stop by his place then and see about getting your car out of the ditch, if he hasn't already done that. Never knew a better man than Jesse. Got a heart bigger than the proverbial size of Texas."

Kaitlyn sucked a deep breath and tried to exhale the guilt that slammed her middle at that last glorified revelation of a man she'd dealt such a cruel blow. All she could do was nod and attempt a smile. She didn't think the smile came through.

As the heavy front door closed, she glanced at Les, and then retreated to the kitchen. After only a few minutes search, she managed a tray of hot chicken noodle soup, a few saltines and some sprite poured over crushed ice. A cup of steaming coffee was included for her.

She set the tray on the lamp table and pulled the covers off of Les's face. "I brought you something to eat. Try to sit up."

He opened his eyes and stared at her face, pain etched into his expresson.

"Where do you hurt, Les?" She felt of his forehead. It seemed a little less hot than last night.

"My bladder is about to explode. Gotta get up—Ahh," he moaned.

Kaitlyn helped him to his feet.

"Did he stop?" Les's voice was low and throaty.

"Who?"

"The guy in the Mac truck that ran me over."

Her laugh was a soft chuckle and she was relieved at his attempt to be funny. "Actually, I ran him down with my sprained ankle and frozen feet. Then I punched him out for you. Feel better?"

He smiled faintly. "Don't make me laugh—I'll wet my pants," he muttered as he headed down the hall.

"Now *that* would be funny," she shot back just before the bathroom door closed.

A couple minutes later, Les sat on the side of the bed and downed a sip of the soup broth and the sprite, only because Kaitlyn had gone to the trouble to fix it for him. He was swimming with nausea before he got his head back down on the pillow.

Les hated the fact that she, of all people, was seeing him in this weakened state. It was bad enough that she had tagged him a loser over the worst mistake of his vet career. That was the last time he'd seen her standing in the barn breezeway at the Grace ranch. It felt like he'd walked around with slumped shoulders for the past three years. No one at the Double OO knew his past, or Kaitlyn's involvement in it. But *she* knew. And here she was, in his backwoods, wound-licking hideout, watching him grovel in a sick bed like a whinny wimp of a man. He hadn't been sick this way in his life. Why now? Just in the nick of time for another round of Kaitlyn Grace, he thought bitterly.

He hadn't thought of the past events with Kaitlyn in a while, not with the usual pain attached to it. But right now, it was all as fresh as the day it happened.

For an instant, he was back in the Grace's barn with raw, unbridled pain in tormented lines screaming across Kaitlyn's face as she drew back and hurled her engagement ring at him. "Get out," she had cried at the top of her lungs. He felt the ring sting his face and he slapped at his forehead to force the too real pressure away. He closed his fingers around the cold, wet cloth that Kaitlyn was just then in process of draping on his feverish head and jerked it off and threw it.

She flinched and moved back a couple of steps before she realized he had been asleep and she'd only startled him. She picked up the cloth and tried to replace it, but he snatched it out of her hands and made a swipe down his face with it.

He felt like a jerk when she turned and walked out of the room.

Les's actions stung. He hadn't been asleep after all. She hadn't considered that he would still be this angry with her. Not after all this time, but this was the second angry move he'd deliberately made toward her. It seemed like a lifetime of one emotional upheaval after another and more than a lifetime of working to bring some semblance of peace and order back to her emotions.

Les Kane had no clue about her struggles since he had disappeared out of Joplin without a word. But then, that's mainly why she had come here. To clue him in on things he needed to know—would *want* to know. This was turning out to be a much harder task than she first thought. So, what else was new?

She re-heated her cup of coffee and sat down at the circular kitchen bar. After only one much needed gulp, the front door opened. It was Judd Luke and a young cowboy who looked like he'd already put in a hard day with mud splatters from his twisted straw hat to his boots. He carried a satchel that spoke *doctor* much louder than he did. She met the two men at the kitchen door.

"Kaitlyn, this is Doctor Cory Raye."

The doctor didn't offer his hand and she sensed a negative vibe aimed her way. Obviously, he didn't care much for his cowboy time being interrupted, but that wasn't her problem.

"Hello. I'm Kaitlyn Grace. Les is in there." She pointed and both men moved toward the bedroom.

Kaitlyn had been there and back with negative people. Her entire life had trained her well to dismiss these rude dudes. At least he came and Les would have professional care. She hoped.

She quietly entered the bedroom and watched as the doctor took his vitals and concluded that Les had a raging case of the flu. He wrote out two prescriptions and handed them to Judd.

"Somebody needs to look in on him, get some liquids in him and make sure he takes this medicine. He'll be down at least a week." He spoke directly to Judd.

Judd nodded and turned to Kaitlyn. "Jesse Brandon said he'd bring your car over here later today. Will you be leaving right away?"

The question caught her off guard. She hadn't had a chance to do what she came for, which was to clean up her guilty past with Les. Before she could think of an answer, Les croaked out an answer for her.

"No. She's not leaving. She's staying here—a few days."

The glare that hit her between the eyes from the sour puss Doc didn't get by her, but she was more concerned with what Les had just said.

Judd looked at her for confirmation that she might be able to look after Les for a few days. There wasn't a judgmental dart on Judd's countenance and Kaitlyn found herself wondering about this big cowboy who prayed so simply, but sincerely, for Les earlier. She thought he must be the kindest man she had ever met.

She looked at Les. He was staring at her with a message she couldn't decipher. Not anger, for sure. Was he asking? Hoping she would stay? She nodded her head, her eyes remaining fixed on Les's a few moments.

"Okay, then," Judd said. "Suppose we let Doc take a look at that ankle while he's here."

"No, thanks. It's fine." She met those kind blue eyes that had such a genuine sparkle and strangely felt herself tear up. "Thank you for everything, Judd. I'll look after Les until he's well."

Doc quickly exited the room without a word.

"I'll get these prescriptions filled and bring them back out here. Les, you behave yourself and get better. We'll be praying for you." Judd nodded at Kaitlyn and left.

Les had closed his eyes and didn't see the tears roll down her cheeks before she walked back to the kitchen. It had dawned on her that she hadn't thought about praying since she was rescued. She also realized she was still parading around in Les's T-shirt and bathrobe. And while her memory was kicked in real good, she remembered that Les had gotten her suitcase out of her car last night. It was in his truck. Then she dejectedly wondered why Dr. Raye had just snubbed her as if he despised her. He didn't know her from Adam or Eve. She knew that was the real reason for the tears.

Okay, Kaitlyn Grace! She inwardly rebuked herself as she wiped the wet off of her face. Enough of that! You're backing up to the old self-condemnation routine when six months in rehab taught you better. Mr. *Hot Shot* Dr. Cory Raye is nothing to you or you to him. And the next time he treats you with such blatant disrespect; you *will* look him in the eye and ask him for an explanation. So there! She patted herself on top of the head, squared her shoulders and headed to the truck to get her clothes.

***

CHAPTER FOUR

After a couple of days, Kaitlyn settled into a routine. She slept on the den couch, fixed liquid meals for Les that he barely touched and gave him his meds on time, which included a sleeping pill.

She forced him to get up and step into a quick warm shower while she changed his bed linens each morning.

It wasn't until the third day that he finally began to eat and drink small amounts.

Judd had brought a thermometer over with the prescriptions to keep track of his temp.

She kept busy by dusting everything within reach and using a tall stool to reach the rest. The Mexican style tiled floors were shining like a new copper penny throughout the house. Laundry, or course, happened every day.

By midmorning on the third day, she pilfered through the kitchen cabinets and found enough ingredients to make a batch of oatmeal raisin cookies with pecan pieces. Who would have thought her favorite cookie stuff could be found in these cabinets.

The spicy aroma wafted down the hall, giving Les reason to drag himself out to inspect what was going on in his house.

When he reached the kitchen door, he stopped and leaned weakly against the door frame. Kaitlyn's back was to him. He watched her dip flour out of his canister; pour small amounts into a large bowl and stir, then repeat the process. He also watched the way she was standing, tight jeans rolled up to mid-calf and one leg bent at the knee and resting on tip toe. She was barefoot and perfectly at ease making what smelled like cookies in his kitchen—and perfectly cute doing it.

And speaking of *his* kitchen, he didn't remember the sparkling shine on everything from ceiling to floor. And that tall glass vase of silk wildflowers that decorated the top of his side by side refrigerator wasn't there before either. Was it?

Lost in his examination of the room, he absently cleared his throat, bringing her around, startled, to face him.

Her gaze traveled slowly over him. His chest was bare of clothes and hair. Black sweat pants hung loosely off of his lean hip bones.

When she got back up to his head, she couldn't stop the slow smile that formed on her lips at the sight of his dark hair sticking up in all directions at once. Had she ever seen a sexier sight in her life? Her hammering heart said no.

Then her practical mind reminded her that Les Kane was part of her past except for the part he didn't know anything about. And that *one* was a large part of why she came here in the first place. Unforeseen circumstances just got in the way of getting this mission completed and in the past as well. So don't get sidetracked, she yelled inside her head!

That's when the spiritual side suddenly jumped up front and center. A compelling, like she hadn't felt in a while, moved over her and drew her attention to the Lord Jesus. She felt as though He was standing shoulder to shoulder beside her and was drawing her to pray. *Lord, please help me do what I need to do here and get it over with.*

"Is that cookies I smell?"

She let out a breath. She was expecting something a little more hostile out of his mouth. "Yes it is. I was just looking for something to do to pass time."

"By the looks of the place, you've managed to keep busy." His eyes stayed fixed on her face.

Her eyes darted around the room, then back. "I hope you don't mind. I've always had a hyper streak."

"So I remember. In fact, I remember most everything about you." His voice was low and a little slurred from his medication. "Let's see...I remember you could ride a horse better than me. I remember you could cook better than Betty Crocker. I remember you were a little rich girl that never acted rich...Just sweet and kind and honest as the day was long, especially about your feelings. You were spot on with that part. When you loved...you went all the way. When you were mad, you threw things. You could sail a shiny little row of diamonds the length of a horse barn and hit the bull's eye, dead center...an expensive little ring of diamonds, at that."

Kaitlyn blinked, trying to stay focused on his face. His words were slicing pieces of her soul away, but she stayed quiet and listened. Partly because she was too shocked to speak and partly because she saw his eyes tear up as his voice grew angrier. But mostly because she realized his face was turning pale as if he might pass out.

Without knowing it, she let the batter-filled spoon splatter onto the tile floor as she ran the few steps to Les and grabbed him around the waist just as his knees began to buckle. She shoved him as tightly as she could against the door frame, pressing herself into him to hold him upright.

"Take a deep breath, Les...deep breath." She heard him suck some air, and then stand up straighter.

"I'm good. Let go."

"I'll let you go when you're beside your bed. Move it, Doc Kane, before I have to twitch my nose and become Nurse Nasty."

He cut his eyes to look down at the top of her head as she headed him down the hall. "Ah, so you're a witch, too. What else are you keeping from me?"

Les stopped suddenly and sniffed. "You better brush up on your hocus pocus, Miss Witch. You just burnt your cookies."

"Oh, no." She dropped her patient and ran back. "Go to bed," she yelled into the oven as she yanked open the door.

Les went to his room grumbling like an old man. "Go to bed...Git up...Take a shower...Eat. Swallow this...Blah, blah, blah." Then he rolled onto his pillow and waited for his head to stop circling the room.

Kaitlyn was flustered as she scraped the charcoaled cookies into the trash can that set inside the broom closet in the laundry room.

After cleaning up the splattered dough and spoon off of the floor, she slid the last batch into the oven, and then took a long breath. One measly sick man walks into the kitchen and her entire cookie making event goes south. Go figure.

She leaned against the cabinet and stared out the window while she waited the ten minutes on the last and only few cookies to bake. Six cookies to be exact. It was silent in the back of the house now, but she had heard all the mumbling before he got out of earshot.

Whine about all my hard work, will he? "I didn't *have* to stay here...Mr. *Belly Acher*," she muttered at the over door as she peeped in on her nicely browning dessert.

"That's right...you didn't. So why *are* you here?" The deep and angry male voice behind her nearly stopped her heart. Then it ticked her off.

She gave him her best murderous glare. "Would you stop sneaking up on me? I thought you went to bed!"

"I can't sleep right now."

"Then just lay there! You don't have your strength back yet. If you pass out on the floor...I can't pick you up."

He looked at her like he hadn't heard a word she said. For a good long minute, they just stared at each other.

Finally, Les softly asked, "Why are you here?"

She pushed a stray lock of hair out of her face. "Because you got sick, "she skirted.

"That's not what I mean and you know it."

She couldn't go there right now. Not like this. The timing wasn't right. So she played a bid for time. "Well...let me see. I was passing through Wyoming and a storm came out of nowhere and my car slid off the road and my dog escaped and I chased him and fell off a cliff and you found me. Can you beat that?" Mischief was smeared across her face.

Les studied her, a gleam of surprise forming on his own face. This was a different Kaitlyn than he remembered—more outspoken, assertive. Notwithstanding her degrading insult of throwing his ring at him the last time he'd seen her. Except for that, she'd always been a little standoffish, quiet—letting her family walk all over her until they finally reduced her to tears. He decided he liked this new and improved version.

He walked one slow step at a time until they stood a breath apart, eyeball to eyeball.

Her face was tilted upward, but staring him down like a bulldog, daring him to be mean to her.

"Yes, I believe I *can* beat that." Les reached up and brushed the back of his hand softly across her cheek, then gently cupped her chin.

She stood still, barely breathing. When his lips lightly pressed hers, they were so hot with fever; Kaitlyn was jerked out of her trance. She pulled back from him. "Les, you're sick!"

That was not the reaction he expected or wanted, but she was right. She didn't need his flu bug. But for some sinister reason, it made him feel much better when he leaned down and so softly whispered in her ear, "Miss Witch...you just burnt your cookies."

Les improved quickly over the next two days. His cabin had turned into a revolving door as visitors, mostly muddy cowboys in spurs and chaps, plodded through at all times of the day. Some of them nodded at her, some winked and some ignored her altogether. Mostly, she stayed out of the way.

When Dr. Raye came by on the fifth day, Kaitlyn decided to take a walk down to the lake. She didn't want to encounter him again, but she needed some fresh air, anyway.

She walked briskly to the short wharf that jutted out into the pond a few yards from the house. But it was far enough to feel a sense of solitude and a few minutes to tuck her emotions back into a nice comfortable place. She sat on the edge of the rough boardwalk and took off her sneakers to dangle her feet in the chilly water.

It irritated her that she had worked so hard putting all her pieces into place through rehab, so faithfully crossing all the T's and dotting the I's. And, through no fault of hers, but sheer fate, the whole deal scrambled just when she was getting to the end of her list.

Half a dozen emotions assaulted her senses, one contradicting the next. She was mad that her neatly tucked-in little world had been yanked loose and hung out like an old rag. It had taken years to repair her damaged psyche and one week to mutilate it. One simple day was all she had needed to offer her genuine heartfelt apology to two men she had hurt. Real emotional pain, dished out by her in ways that couldn't be taken back.

Jesse Brandon was so obviously angry with her and yet, basically forced to help get her car fixed. She hadn't seen his face since the night he'd helped rescue her. He had sent a message through Judd Luke about her Toyota needing extensive repairs, as well as asking her permission for Bonnie to remain with Hank and Martha Walton until she was better able to deal with her. Everyone had heard that Les was sick and she was taking care of him. Actually, she was very grateful to the Walton's for their help, and Jesse, too.

And Dr. Cory Raye. Now there was a piece of man work! Just where did he get off treating her like a disease!

She kicked her toes upward from the water and splashed herself in the face. The shock of cold water felt like God saying, *Take a breath, Kaitlyn. Cool off!* She knew she was wallowing, but sometimes it just felt good.

But this *thing* with Les had left her bewildered. A couple of days ago, something had happened between them. Les had shown his anger at her more than once, and then kissed her. Maybe he was just lonely and she was convenient. He'd made it impossible for her to leave after he got sick by telling Judd and Dr. Raye that she was staying a few days.

She lowered her head and stared into the rippling flare on the water, as thoughts continued to wash her mind. There was Bonnie, the storm, then her car sliding out of control and her fall off the edge of the world—and Les—and Jesse. And where was God? She really wasn't looking to find fault with God in all these dramatics about her past week of life, but she did wonder where He fit in to the mess. Hadn't she asked Him to lead her steps just before the bottom fell out? Literally.

She kicked the water again, then slid wet toes into her shoes and headed back to the edge of the wharf and onto the grass without looking up. When she did look up, she almost fell backward at the sight of Jesse Brandon sitting on a lathered sorrel. If nothing else, she should have heard the heavy breathing of the horse before she nearly bumped into his massive soapy chest.

She slapped her hand over her pounding heart. *Doesn't anybody around here know how to yell hello before they sneak up and scare the daylights out of a person,* she wanted to screech up at him, but his hard silent stare stopped time—and her mouth. She didn't have a word in it.

They just stared at each other for several long seconds before Jesse finally chipped the ice.

"Kaitlyn Grace? Is that your name?"

Shame rolled through her until she could only nod her head. Her eyes wouldn't move from his as bad as she wanted to hang her head and walk away. Or better yet, vaporize into thin air.

She watched him slowly swing his leg over the saddle and dismount. Through the caked dust on his face, she saw his lips pull into a half smile, the expression in his eyes matching it. There was no anger here.

Jesse slid a dirty leather glove off of his right hand and added it to the gloved hand holding the horse's reins before he stepped to within arm's reach and extended his bare hand to her.

"I don't believe we've met...Jesse Brandon."

Kaitlyn took his hand, then quickly let go. Was he mocking her?

"Guess you got the message that your car would be a few days in the shop?"

Again she could only nod. Tears were burning her eyelids. Finally, she couldn't keep up the pretense he had started.

"Jesse..." She hesitated, straining at the fullness in her throat. "I'm so...sorry..."

His hand came up to indicate *stop*, then shook his head. That half smile was still on his face. "No need for that, Katie... Kaitlyn. You were a kid having fun and I was an immature idiot. Let's just leave it at that."

She swallowed as much of the guilt that would go down. "If you don't mind, I *need* to apologize for what I did to you. That's one of the reasons I came to Wyoming."

Jesse's face only flickered with surprise, but the gentleness was still intact. He stood quietly while she struggled to get through the moment.

"I won't bore you with details unless you decide you want them. I'm just truly sorry for the way I handled myself...the way I treated you."

"It's been over for me for a long time. I accept your apology and no hard feelings on my part. Are we squared away on this now?"

She opened her mouth to say more, but the pickup coming into the clearing got both of their attention.

Kaitlyn glanced up to see Jesse's face take on an urgent crease. When he walked off leading his horse toward the truck, she followed, surprised when the truck parked and a small boy jumped out of the driver's side.

"Dad! Dad!" The boy ran to Jesse in a panic. "It's mom. She's laying on the kitchen floor and can't get up. The baby might be coming out and our phone won't work. Granny Martha is with her and said to hurry and find you."

Jesse started to mount his horse, and then jerked his head up at Kaitlyn. "Here...take care of Boss for me," and chunked the reins toward her. "Get in, Andy."

Everything was tumbling through Jesse's mind at once. He remembered that Katie...Kaitlyn, had been a good hand with a horse and why in God's name was his eight year old son driving his old ranch truck on the highway and his wife was giving birth to his son in the kitchen floor? And what was he thinking, going off to help chase calves, with his wife due two weeks ago? And what in blazes happened to the phone line?

He saved all the questions for later and drove the old six banger like he was competing at the Indianapolis 500.

Kaitlyn was shocked at the whole incident, but thrilled at the new four-legged charge she had just acquired. She watched Jesse back the truck out and disappear through the trees. Andy? That was Jesse's son? He had to be around ten years old. And his wife was having a baby. No wonder Jesse was so pleasant. He's a very happy family man. She couldn't keep from smiling. *Lord, take care of Jesse's wife and baby. Let them be safe.*

"Well, Mr. Boss...wonder what I'm supposed to do with you?"

During her moment of contemplative indecision, the heavy door of the house opened and Les stepped out on the porch. She guessed his string of visitors had ended. He leaned against a log column, looking across the yard at her, obviously recognizing the horse.

"Do you need some help with Boss. He must have got loose from one of the boys," he said casually, thinking the gelding had just wandered up.

She led the tired pony closer to the porch. "Actually, Jesse Brandon was riding him. His little son drove up and said his mom was having a baby...so I got thrown the reins and told to take care of him. I really don't know what...

Les looked confused. "Now, *what?*" He interrupted. *"Who* drove up and said..."

"Andy. He called Jesse dad and said his mom was in the kitchen floor and couldn't get up."

Les turned and raced into the house. Inside of a minute he was back with his jeans and boots on and pulling a T-shirt over his head as he ran to his dually. In seconds, he was gone.

Kaitlyn stared dumbfounded at Les's sudden strength of body and disappearance around the bend of trees. She looked Boss in the eye and back at the emptied yard, realizing she had been left alone to deal with a tired and hungry horse. She could feel the heat radiating from his still heaving body, smell the horse sweat that was anything but offensive. In fact, the hot, sweaty smell of Boss filled her senses with an intense longing that she thought had left her years ago.

She had let all of her father's horses go to new owners, including her beloved Melody, who went to a little four year old girl who wanted nothing in the whole world except a horse. The black spotty mare was more than just Kaitlyn's horse. She was her friend, her salvation from the unbearable loneliness of her youth. Kaitlyn called her Melody because her presence in her life was like a song in her heart. The smells of the barn, the feed, the leather, the horse sweat and pine shavings always gave her a sense of belonging somewhere—sense of being loved.

The horses had always responded to her presence with knickers and excited dancing, all wanting her attention. Melody was allowed to meander around the ranch, loose and free in her older years, but always came trotting up as soon as Kaitlyn's voice reached her on the wind.

It suddenly felt like a new wind had softly breezed over her as she stood there beside Boss, remembering. And suddenly, she missed having a horse and the lifestyle that came with it.

She sighed heavily and stroked Boss's wet, dirty face. "Well, young man...let's go see if we can find a pen and bucket of grain for all your obvious hard work."

Only slightly unnerved because Boss was a stranger and it had been a long time since she'd ridden, Kaitlyn mounted up. Her feet were a far cry from resting in the saddle stirrups, but she squeezed her knees on both sides and signaled her ride to walk on. The rush of joy that seized her heart and mind surprised her. This was where she had found love and acceptance most of her life. This was where she felt a peace that she doubted she could put into words, even to herself. Right here, on the back of a horse.

Without a clue, the pair followed the well tracked road. Actually it was Kaitlyn who didn't have a clue, but she knew Boss did. She threw him his full head and let him take her on the most invigorating walk/ride she'd had in years.

The fall air was crispy perfect, many leaves were changing color, the pines smelled like Christmas. Had she stepped up onto the precipice of Heaven, this is what it would be like. She was sure of it.

The road wound around the countryside at least a half mile before she spotted a ranch spread through a scenic valley. A log house that could pass for one she'd see on Log Home magazine's cover caught her eye first, and then the equally fancy barn just below the back of the house.

Boss took her inside the wide barn door and stopped in front of the tack room. Kaitlyn sat still and listened. The place was deserted, except for some noisy pony banging a feed bucket around in one of the stalls.

"Hello?" she called out.

Satisfied that she was on her own, she dismounted, patted Boss, and whispered softly to him as she pulled off his saddle and pad. She set the saddle on one of the dozen empty saddle racks in the tack room and draped the pad, bottom side up, to dry, then fished a brush out of a tub of grooming supplies.

After replacing the bridle and bit with a soft nylon halter, she rewarded his day with a thorough brushing. The wash rack was beside the tack room, where she dropped his rope and ran warm water over his legs and feet. The gelding turned his head and looked at her as if to say *thanks*, then he walked down the barn alleyway and stopped at the door of an empty stall and waited. Kaitlyn slid open the gate and he went inside, dropped and rolled in the clean shavings. Intelligence oozed out of this pony. She laughed at him. "No place like home...huh, Boss man."

"Are you sure about that?"

The sullen sneer behind her brought her around to face it, heart racing. *One more person sneaks up on me and I won't be held responsible for unmercifully clobbering them!*

Kaitlyn gaped at the man who had suddenly appeared behind her. Dr. Cory Raye. His eyes were cold.

With great effort she composed herself and attempted a smile. "Oh...you scared me. I didn't know anyone else was here." Then it struck her. "Is this your ranch?"

"No. It's Judd Luke's place. What are you doing here?"

"I brought Boss home for Jesse. He had an emergency and left his horse with me. But we got along fine. Boss showed me right where he belonged." She tried to lighten the air, but it wasn't working. He was glaring at her.

She straightened her back, deciding it was time to bite the bullet with this guy. With hands on her hips, she looked at the concrete for a few seconds, then back into his eyes. "Dr. Raye, do you have something against me? You've been unfriendly since we met and I can't for the life of me..."

"You don't remember me, do you?" he interrupted.

That surprised her and she squinted at him, trying to recognize something. Of course she didn't recognize him. How would she know him? "Where should I remember you from?" Humor creased her expression, knowing he was about to be embarrassed at an obvious mistaken identity.

"You paid me for the service of helping you leave a friend of mine standing at the alter some time back. Hush money, I believe it was...Except I didn't know that was your reason for needing an immediate ride to the airport."

Kaitlyn went still, eyes rounded, before her hand went to her open mouth. "That was you?" She was mortified.

His laugh was mocking and cruel. "Didn't occur to me to ask what I was really getting paid for." He drew his wallet out of his back pocket and pulled out a one hundred dollar bill. "Here." He thrust the bill toward her. "Take this off my conscience."

When she didn't move to take it, Cory stepped closer and stuck the crisp paper down the neckline of her shirt.

Speechless, humiliation wrapped her like a strait jacket.

The doctor walked away. She heard his spurs jingle with every step down the concrete breezeway until the sound faded away.

Her stomach felt like a man-sized fist was stuck in the middle of it, her blood like it had curdled in her veins. She pulled the money out of her shirt and let the bill float to the floor. A soft nicker from the stall reminded her to feed Boss. A feed room with an automatic door closer was next to the tack room. Mindlessly, she scooped out grain and peeled off a flake of grass hay, saw that his water bucket was full, and then walked out of the barn.

Trying hard didn't work to put a lid on her rioting emotions. Her thoughts were too scattered to pull herself together. One foolish mistake, years ago, seemed to have been laying for her—waiting for the chance to pay her back. She thought she would get a grip on herself quicker if she could cry it out. But there were no tears. Just rage.

She walked toward Les's cabin, but not on the road. She crossed into the woods, not wanting to encounter anyone on her way back. It seemed that every move she made on this well intentioned trip had blown up in her face.

She walked with a brisk determination to put her encounter with Cory out of her mind. Hopefully, by the time she got back, Les wouldn't be able to see any sign of her anger. She didn't want to think about it. Ever again! And she didn't want to go there with Les.

Then for the first time, she wondered if Les knew what had taken place between her and Jesse back when. Did he know she had actually planned to marry Jesse Brandon after a two week fling on the rebound from her breakup with him?

Kaitlyn stopped to catch her breath, now that she had stomped most of her anger out. The fact that she'd been engaged to two men within weeks of each other never occurred to her in that particular context. If Les knew about that, he would not have wanted her near him, much less insisted she stay in his cabin and take care of him.

What kind of woman does that?

The huge evil fist felt like it had buried itself even deeper into the middle of her gut. She bent forward slightly, feeling sick.

She had come to terms with so many aspects of her life, from her early childhood until now. She had accepted that her parents never loved her and subsequently brought on so much of the self-deprecating events throughout her life. She got that. She had reached the other side of so much self-hatred. This Wyoming trip was only the end, the finishing up of years of the healing process to her damaged soul. So what was this sudden loathing that was threatening to cut off her air? She felt like she was choking.

Then the dam burst. She sunk to her knees trembling as painful sobs sucked at the oxygen in her lungs.

She knew. From the moment she had opened her eyes and saw Les in real-time and flesh on the cliff ledge and not just in her dreams, she knew. She loved him. She wanted nothing in this world except to be with the one love of her life. The one that she knew, in the deepest part of her knower, she was meant to share this life with. But he didn't yet know her terrible secrets. She was sure he didn't know about Jesse. That would be enough to cause him to despise her, if that was the only thing. But it wasn't. She had to tell him about the baby. About his son. That one, Les would never forgive her for.

Kaitlyn hung her head and cried with overwhelming despair. *Jesus, help me,* she whispered through racking sobs.

A long time later, she was in the same spot on the ground, but sitting cross-legged and staring serenely into the maze of trees and brush around her. She had stopped crying a while ago, but didn't feel like moving. There seemed to be an almost unnatural calm enveloping her entire body. Her mind and body was cocooned in warmth, a weightless kind of peace. She just sat still; basking in her Father's loving care. He had heard her cry for help and had restored her crumbling strength. There was nothing anywhere on the earth to compare with this heavenly brand of peace, a stillness of mind and body, until you could only praise Him and continue to drink it in.

Les drove slowly back to the Double OO, a dozen thoughts rushing him at once.

Thankfully, Laura Brandon didn't seem to be hurt or in labor. She had slipped in spilled water, but managed to break her fall without going down full force on her bottom. He had helped Jesse get her up and in the truck so they could visit the doctor in Jackson for a precautionary checkup. With Hank and Martha Walton to care for the kids, he headed back home.

Les rubbed his face up and down, and then threaded his fingers through his hair. He still wasn't feeling up to par, but regardless, he needed to deal with Kaitlyn's sudden appearance in his Wyoming space.

That was something he could never really lay claim to. His own space.

He wondered, for the first time in years, about his parents. He had no idea who they were. The story he was told didn't leave any clue to their identities or his. His mother, it was assumed it was her, had left him as a newborn at the fire station in Kansas City, Missouri. His first four years were spent in a foster home and the next fourteen in a state orphanage.

After high school, at age eighteen, he was shown the door to fend for himself. He was named by his foster parents and carried their last name. But in the midst of the legal process to adopt him, they divorced and he was taken away by the state.

Les raked a hand through his hair again. The sun was going down and his fever was rising. The cool air almost hurt his hot skin and he rolled up his truck window.

He realized this late model dually he was driving was probably the only true space he could call his own. He had paid cash for it after living pillow to post and working two and three jobs at a time to get himself through vet school. Those days were hard. More nights than he wanted to remember were spent in a public shelter or a public rest room. But by sheer determination and a lot of grit, he made it.

He recalled the night he walked across that stage and received his diploma. He had no place to go home to afterward. No family to applaud him, to be proud of him. He walked from the auditorium back to the city's homeless shelter and cried all the way. He was so tired, so relieved and so lonely.

Within a month, he was hired by an old veterinarian from Joplin, whom he'd met getting coffee in McDonalds. He took

Les under his wing and taught him old school doctoring to go along with his up-to-date schooling.

Les smiled as he remembered Dr. Southerland. He was a rough talking old coot. He died only after a few months of taking Les on, but he had given him a foot up to becoming a good, well-rounded animal doctor. In short order, Les rented an apartment and bought a good used pickup.

Then he met Kaitlyn on a call to her family's horse barn. It was love at first sight for him. And she had loved him, too. There was no way to fake that light that shimmered in her eyes every time she had looked at him. She adored him then. She had given every inch of her body to him, *only* him.

And that earth shaking love that he had briefly shared with her was the same one that gutted him and left him bleeding for the past long years.

***

CHAPTER FIVE

Les walked in his front door and pulled off his boots, expecting to find Kaitlyn doing laundry or cooking something. She seemed to hunt for things to do. He closed the door behind him and headed down the hall toward the bedroom. The house was too quiet. He stopped and listened intently. All he could hear was empty and cold.

"Katie?" he called, but no answer. He figured she had gone down to the pond, but he didn't bother to look. He was feeling lousy and stretched out on his bed, fully dressed.

Sleep claimed him immediately, but then, he popped awake. He lifted his head and turned his eyes toward the window. It was pitch dark outside. *What time is it?* The digital read 9 PM. *Oh man, I must have slept like a dead man.* It had been three hours since he laid down.

The house was dark and still silent. He made his way to the kitchen turning on lights as he went. When he saw the couch unoccupied, he became alarmed. Why wasn't Katie in the house yet?

Then he remembered that she had been left with Jesse's mount, Boss. He went out and walked toward the pond, then glanced around the back of the cabin, squinting into the darkness. Had she decided to go for a ride and gotten lost? Did the auto shop deliver her car and she left. But then, what would she have done with the horse?

He turned a circle and scratched his head, then went back in and put on his boots and hat just inside the front door. For the second time today, he forgot how sick he felt.

Before he climbed into his truck, he yelled out, "Kaitlyn!" into the darkness several times in all directions. Not even his echo came back.

That horse, he reasoned, knows where he belongs. Maybe Katie is at the ranch barn hanging out. That would be her thing. At least it used to be.

The first time he'd laid eyes on her, she was prissing around in tight jeans and knee-high western boots like a little barn queen. He'd never seen anything so sexy in his life. In fact, he had gotten the impression that day that she had dressed just for him and knew the effect she was having on him. He laughed out loud remembering those long eyelashes batting over her eyes that were half closed and slanted up at him. He'd wanted her from that moment. And now!

He stopped the rambling thoughts because he felt such confusion about...*now*. He needed to locate her and have that *why are you here* conversation—not sit here and deliberately set himself up for more heartache.

The usual night lights were on in the barn. Judd's hauler was the only vehicle still there. As Les walked to the center of the breezeway, his spurs jingled his presence.

Judd stepped out of the tack room, surprise lighting his face when he saw Les. He came forward extending his hand. "Well...I see the Almighty is still in the business of raising the dead. Good to see you out, Les."

"Thanks. I was just making sure Boss got put up all right," he hedged around his real concern.

"Boss?" Judd headed for the gelding's stall and looked downward through the bars. "He's laying down in here." Judd's eyes narrowed on Les in contemplation. "Is there a problem?"

"No, I thought Kaitlyn might be here. She obviously rode him over here earlier. Jesse had a small emergency at home and left her holding his reins."

"He's bedded down in there, but I haven't seen Kaitlyn. I've been here about an hour."

"All right...well, I'm sure she'll show up. Maybe she got a lift to town to see about her car." Les tried to sound nonchalant, but his insides had twisted in a tight wad.

As Les turned to leave, Judd said suddenly, "Wait a minute," and disappeared into the tack room. He returned in seconds holding up a one hundred dollar bill. "This was found by A.J. laying almost in front of Boss's stall. None of the boys claimed it, so I'm thinking Kaitlyn might have dropped it, now that I know she was here today. Take it and ask her if she lost it. That's a lot of money to misplace."

Les hesitantly took the bill and left.

It was all she could do to talk herself out of a bloodcurdling panic. Kaitlyn hated the dark. But this was worse than dark. She was lost in the Wyoming woods, hardly able to see her hand in front of her face. How could she have sat down out here and fallen asleep?

She was cold and terrified. What happened to that glorious moment she'd just spent swimming in the peace of God. Did she just enjoy a sweet dream only to awaken to a hellish nightmare, alone in the inky black wilderness, with no idea which way to go? She stood, squinting into the night trying to get a grip on what to do. She couldn't see more than a few inches around her. Clouds blocked the stars and moon.

For a minute she was back on the ledge with wind and rain raging around her. Only this time, the storm was a black silence with fear trying to drown her. She was afraid to move and afraid not to. What if she headed deeper into the dark woods? What if she ran face first into a bear? Who even knew she was missing? Mountain lions lived in this area. *Oh, God!* She couldn't move. She was paralyzed. *Oh, God!*

Les strode through the house, checking every room, turning on every light that wasn't already burning. When he spied her suitcase on the floor beside the couch, he knew for sure something was wrong. She didn't leave.

His nerves were throbbing with tension as he paced from the living room to the kitchen, knowing she was in trouble, somewhere. *Katie, blast it! Where are you?*

Without particularly deciding to, he turned on his heel and walked quickly through the kitchen and utility room and out the back door. He had raked his hand across the outside light switch on the wall as he went out, but the bulb was burned out. He stood a few feet out in the back yard staring into the dark space and yelled, "Kait...lyn!"

He listened until his voice faded away, and then called again. Then, again.

Kaitlyn's eyes grew big when she thought she heard her name faintly way off in the distance. She tried to call out, but fear held her throat closed. Then she heard it again, more distinctly.

"Les." His name came out in a whisper, but when she heard her name again, she pushed "Les" out through a high pitched scream.

He heard his name screamed from the blackness of the trees. The sound was not that far away. He turned and ran into the house and grabbed a flashlight off of the kitchen bar. Thank God she hadn't stuck it someplace where he couldn't find it.

He ran into the thick brush and trees for several yards, then stopped and called again. "Kait...lyn!"

"Les! Come get me. Les!"

"Keep calling, Katie. I need to follow your voice," he yelled. He had to keep the flashlight beam on the ground at his feet to see where to walk.

"Les! Over here! I'm here!"

Finally, a tiny stream of yellow light pierced her blackness.

"Talk to me, Katie."

"Here. Over here." Her voice broke into a sob of sheer relief when Les reached her. She threw herself into his arms and cried, hanging on to him with a strength that a pry bar couldn't loosen.

He wrapped his arms tightly around her until she began to calm down. "It's all right, baby...I've got you." He pressed her head against his chest, and then soothingly rubbed his hand down her hair. "I've got you," he whispered. Oh, dear Jesus, she felt so good in his arms.

His six foot four frame swallowed her as she slumped her body against his; pushing into him as though he might attempt to move out of her grasp. Not a chance. The memory of her smell and feel was intoxicating, opening every raw nerve of his past and soothing the pain of it with the tight, needy grasp she held onto him with—a grasp that clenched around his middle for all she was worth, yet making him realize, once again, how small and fragile she was.

It didn't matter anymore about the past. What happened—happened. He knew it would be after the battle that he would ever let her go from his life again. She was where she belonged. He knew that as well as he knew his sanity could very well be on the line if she didn't feel the same for him.

She raised her head to look up at him. Their eyes held each other, faces almost in silhouette against the darkness. "I've never been so scared in my life," she whispered.

He wanted to tell her she would never be afraid again because he wasn't leaving her alone, ever. Instead, "You're safe now. Let's get back to the house before we calm down enough to feel the cold air."

Kaitlyn knew a change had occurred in their relationship. Looking into Les's eyes in those short moments revealed nothing of the anger he had harbored all these years. He was obviously relieved that she was safe. The tenderness in his eyes was the gentle Les she had met and fallen in love with.

For the first time, she fully believed that this trip to Wyoming to see Les was not just because his name was on a, *to do* list, made up at rehab. No, there was a settling in her heart that this was a pre-planned *God* trip. Not just to say *I'm sorry* to a few folks and move on, but to bring her back full circle to the place where she was supposed to be in the first place, with Les Kane.

They made their way back to the cabin, Les's arm securely around her shoulders and her arm wrapped tightly around his waist. Not a word was spoken as they followed the small splatter of light at their feet.

Les's spirits had risen to a bursting high at what he'd seen in Kaitlyn's eyes. It had been a very long time since he'd felt this *love* high. He liked it and full well meant to keep it.

An hour later, Kaitlyn had showered and was fixing a light supper of tomato soup and pimento cheese sandwiches while Les got cleaned up.

She had been so enamored with the sweet revelation of possibly beginning anew with Les, that the come down devastated her nearly to tears. She hadn't been thinking clearly. Everything she had dreamed of having in her life was within reach until she floated back to earth and remembered. Les wanted to talk to her after supper tonight. He wanted to know why she was in Wyoming in the first place. And the answers to all of that would change how he felt about her. It would be all over before she had a chance to begin. There was no way to explain what she had done, to make him feel anything but disgust and a new, more devastating hatred of her. There was no way Les's reborn feelings for her could survive if he knew what she had done.

Tears of hopeless misgivings slid down her cheeks before she could blot them away. Until that moment, she'd had every intention of laying all of the events of her life at Les's feet; telling him the full truth of everything, and then returning to her ranch in Joplin to begin life all over again. That was the plan laid out in her notebook that she'd been required to keep at rehab. All of it had been accomplished. Even her new addition to the list, Jesse Brandon, was thankfully and peacefully finished.

Only Les was left. And only more pain and brokenness could result now if she followed through with all of the details. He had a right to know things, but she had a right to be happy and fulfilled for a change. And so did Les.

She heard him walk into the kitchen behind her and sit down at the half moon-shaped bar. His soup and sandwich was waiting on him and she sat across from him with hers. This was a first, their sharing a meal together in the kitchen. Neither spoke. They ate with only the sounds of spoons clanging soup bowls. The air was heavy with silent thoughts, wars waging in two minds, vying for an opening to put the past to rest and lay aside the malice and pride that had wasted far too much of their lives already.

Kaitlyn got up to gather the dishes. Les quickly got up to step around the end of the bar and gather Kaitlyn into his arms. He tried to pull her against him gently, pull her face up to his by the back of her hair, slow and easy. But the years were long and his need to touch her was overwhelming. He knew he hadn't succeeded in the *gentle* department when he heard a startled intake of breath as his lips claimed hers.

Somewhere in the middle of his needy rush, he managed to pull back and slow down. His hands cradled her face. Her skin was as soft as he remembered, her green eyes wanting with a desperate plea to be loved and cherished by somebody. That somebody would be him. It was meant to be him. He just knew that. And he believed that she knew it, too.

"You were crying when I came into the kitchen. What made you cry?" He whispered into her hair.

"You. This."

He kissed her nose, her eyes—the side of her face. "That's what I thought. Don't cry anymore. Everything will be okay."

She reached up then and softly ran the tip of her fingers over his cheek, not sure what to do now. How much to reveal without losing it all, again. The loss would be for good next time. They had to take time to heal the wounds that were already there. She knew now that she couldn't tell him the whole truth without destroying this brand new second chance they were trying to find with each other.

She sighed heavily and dropped her head into the crook of his arm. Exhaustion took her over suddenly. Her emotions, particularly the paralyzing fear she'd experienced out in the dark woods a short time ago, had caught up with her.

Les still had not gotten his questions answered, but that would have to wait one more night. He abruptly grasped her hand and started towards the hallway, pulling her with him. "Come on. You're going to sleep in my bed tonight. I doubt if you've had a decent night's rest since you've been here."

She didn't hesitate, but hated that she was putting him on the couch again. She knew he still needed another day or two to be fully recuperated from his illness.

"The sheets are still clean," he told her. "I've hardly been in bed today since you changed them. And I'll take care of cleaning up the kitchen."

Les helped her to sit on the side of the bed. He could tell she was about to cry again. It was no wonder. She'd had a full load of trauma since he discovered she was in the area. When hell decides to break loose, he thought, it comes in by the truck load.

She looked up at him, her eyes flooding. "Les, I...can't take your bed. You..."

"Just lay down, Katie. You need rest. We'll talk tomorrow."

When her head hit the pillow, he straightened the top sheet and quilt and covered her. He turned her light out, then went back to the kitchen and made short order of putting it back together. Normally he wouldn't have bothered with cleaning up tonight, but Kaitlyn had been so careful to keep everything in the house clean.

Fact was, he had no intention of sleeping on the couch. He intended to crawl under the covers with Katie and wrap her up in his arms—arms that had been aching to hold her for several long years. He needed her. And whether she would admit it or not, she needed him—to shield her from a real or imagined enemy—to make her laugh and hold her when she cried—to help her accomplish her dreams—to love her when she was right and when she was wrong.

She was sound asleep when he shucked his clothes down to underwear and T-shirt and slid in bed beside her. His arm reached around her middle and pulled her snugly into the bend of his body.

Realization trickled through her deep-sleep dreams until she finally got what was happening and tried to rise up. "Les? No, I can't. I don't..."

"Shush, it's okay. Just let me hold you while you sleep. That's all." He felt her relax as his large, warm hand gently caressed her hair away from her face.

Fully awake now, she felt the length of his body curled around hers like a safe harbor. It was amazing how safe she felt. Like nothing could ever breach the barrier of his strength to hurt or scare her again. And she was fully aware at that moment that a decision had been reached in her mind—a choice that, right or wrong, she had just accepted responsibility for the consequences as well. She would not tell Les, not yet, her most devastating secret. She could not take a chance on losing him again when their feelings were so fragile and new. Not yet. His *knowing* about his son couldn't change the facts. Nothing could ever correct what she had done.

She began to cry, but without a sound. The memory was too hard to bring back, the pain too great. Lying in Les Kane's arms, the father of her baby son suddenly became a bittersweet moment that felt worse than being all alone with the memory.

He felt her body tense up against him and figured she was reliving those fearful hours in the woods tonight. That, along with extreme exhaustion, was probably playing havoc with her emotions.

He tightened his hold and shortly they both fell into an exhausted sleep.

Kaitlyn awoke to the smell of bacon. A glance toward the window told her it was *way* too early for this. The stars were still twinkling. But the aroma of strong coffee dripping wafted through the bedroom door, drawing her up out of a hard, deep sleep. She had learned to drink coffee hanging around her family's horse barn on early winter mornings before the school bus arrived. No one ever noticed that she bellied up to the coffee pot along with the ranch crew. Or else, no one cared except, maybe, Tack, a farrier who mentioned once that if she kept it up, she'd grow hair on her chest. Funny how certain things will stick in a person's memory like that.

It took a couple minutes for her to get fully awake enough to recall that she hadn't slept alone. That recall was enough to bring her fully alert.

She lay there imagining she could still feel the weight of Les's arm draped over her. She wasn't ready for that feeling to go away. The sweet innocence of their bodies cuddled together all night. He probably had no idea how desperately she needed what he had given her. It felt like the arms of destiny had reached around her and filled her full of hope.

She got up and followed her nose and coffee habit to the kitchen via the bathroom. The kitchen was empty. Bacon and scrambled eggs were on a plate on top of the stove, coffee steaming in the Mr. Coffee pot, but no Les.

Her eye hit a notepad lying beside the toaster where two slices of bread were stuck in each slot waiting to become toast. The note was written clearly, in a nice handwriting. *Had to get back in the saddle. Thanks for letting me hold you last night. I look forward to tonight. Les*

Her knees got weak and she held on to the edge of the counter top. *Lord Jesus, can this really be happening? Are You giving me a second chance?*

She poured a cup of coffee and sat down at the bar. A smile of pure joy tugged at her lips. She felt as if she had been made love to all night. But Les had only wrapped her up in his arms and sandwiched her away from her heartaches.

Kaitlyn considered herself a totally independent woman. God knew she had earned that badge. But her self-acclaimed liberty to stand strong as an individual didn't feel threatened in the least—Enhanced, maybe. Perfected, like the missing piece of a puzzle put in place. If she climbed one step higher in happiness, she knew she and that cup of coffee in her hand would explode into a million bits. *"Dear Lord Jesus,"* she whispered, *"thank You for ordering my steps back to Les. Help me get it right this time."*

She sat still and concentrated on the One she was talking to, praising Him over and over from the depths of her being. From somewhere within that profound place, words she had never heard before rose up. She became quiet, almost tranquilized as she heard: **Bone of my bones, flesh of my flesh.**

She held her breath at the sound of those words filtering through her mind. She had no idea what that meant, but she *knew* that her Heavenly Father had just spoken to her.

SURRENDERED III

The moment seemed to fade away, leaving her feeling very calm and peaceful, yet not having a clue what to do now. But, it appeared, she had all day to do it.

***

CHAPTER SIX

Les pulled at the brim of his battered straw Stetson, then got a second bite on the strand of barbed wire, clamped it tight and pumped the pullers until the wire was taut enough to saw a tree. "That bull gets out of *this* fence again, he's gonna have to be one tough hoss," Les muttered to his horse, who wasn't particularly listening from where he was tied to the back end of the old ranch work truck.

Les had just tied off the last broken strand when he heard horses pounding the ground toward him. He straightened up and watched the ranch boss, Judd Luke, and Cory Raye, rein to a stop six feet from him. "Looks like the two of you timed it just right," Les joked with mock sarcasm.

"Yeah, well, we were all wondering how long you were going to play sick. That little gal must have headed for new territory, huh?" Cory bit back at him.

The comment came out a little too sharp for Les. He turned to look at him straight on. "Why do you say that?"

Cory shrugged and pursed his lips. "Because women like that are on every street corner in Jackson. She didn't have a problem taking up with you out here in the sticks."

Judd saw a dangerous light jump into Les's eyes and brought the conversation back to business. "Les, load your tools back up in the truck and leave it set right there. Ride on out beyond the back ninety a ways and you'll find some of the boys. There's a few strays still missing. Doc and I will be at the barn." With that he turned his horse around and left, Cory following.

Les stood for a while watching them ride off. If Cory, or Judd, for that matter, thought this was finished, they were mistaken. He knew Judd would have been out on the roundup today, but chose to take Cory out of his line of fire. However, if it cost him his job, Les vowed to look the doctor up later.

The ride back to the Double OO barn was silent except for the horses clip clomping. Judd didn't know what that remark about Kaitlyn Grace was all about, but he did feel obligated to keep a peaceful atmosphere for his working cowboys when possible. And that chore was usually always possible. A deliberate troublemaker that couldn't be reckoned with was shown the Double OO gate without hesitation.

But Doc Raye was a different situation. Sort of. He came out to the Luke's ranch mostly for a little cowboy fun. He liked the ranching lifestyle, but he had recently begun a full time career as a family doctor. His fully staffed clinic was in downtown Jackson Hole.

Dr. Raye, known around the ranch as Cory, had worked off and on for Jesse Brandon's dude ranch while he paid his way through medical school. He'd been around for several years. But this uncalled for lambasting he'd just done to Les Kane needed to be addressed.

Judd's curiosity got up a little at what might have prompted Cory's derogatory remarks about a strange young woman from out of state needing a few days help. And she certainly gave back as much as she got by taking care of Les while he was down sick with the flu.

Of course, Judd wasn't born yesterday. He wasn't a fool. It wouldn't have set well with him for Les to be shacking up in the foreman's quarters. But these circumstances were understandable, the way things happened.

Judd's ordained minister's license was not taken lightly. He, above all the others on his ranch, had to uphold his convictions to do what pleased the Lord Jesus. The church services held in his home on the Double OO would be nothing short of hypocritical otherwise. He strived daily to simply please his Heavenly Father.

He dismounted inside the barn and tied his haltered horse inside a stall. Cory unsaddled and brushed his mount before turning him loose in the pen next to it. The two men met in the middle of the breezeway.

Judd motioned his arm toward Cory's horse. "Does this mean you're done for the day?"

"Yeah. I know you meant to help with the round up so I'll let you get on with your work. I get that I'm holding you up."

Cory started to leave, then turned back to face his friend. "Look, Judd, I wasn't trying to start trouble out there. I was just putting a bug in Les's ear about that woman. He doesn't know what he's getting mixed up with."

Judd's eyes narrowed. "Would you mind explaining what you mean? Sounds like you know her."

"I do. I had some dealings with her back a few years ago over at Jesse's place."

"At High Point? A few years ago?"

Cory nodded. "Ever hear the story of the little gal that Jesse was supposed to marry some years ago? Her name was Katie."

Judd nodded, not making the connection. "Yes, I knew about that. She left without a word to him or anybody, as I recall."

"Kaitlyn Grace is Katie. Same girl that jilted Jesse."

Judd's eyes widened and then narrowed with a frown while he assembled that shocking revelation in his head. "Are you sure about this?"

"As sure as I'm standing here talking to you. She came out where I was painting fence for Jesse that day and paid me one hundred dollars to stop what I was doing and drive her to the airport in Jackson. Course, I jumped at the chance to make a hundred dollars for a quick run to town. Didn't learn till later that I had helped the little tart to break Jesse's heart for him."

Judd studied him a moment, and then shook his head in disbelief. Not at Cory, because he did seem to know what he was talking about. He simply realized what a ticking bomb this situation could be.

"So, does Les know about her past with Jesse?" Judd asked, still frowning.

"Don't know. But I made sure she remembered me yesterday when she was putting Jesse's horse up for him, which doesn't make sense to me. What was she doing with Jesse yesterday?"

There were quite a few unanswered questions, Judd realized. "Well, we shouldn't be jumping to conclusions. I agree, it's confusing, but I suggest we let Les handle his own personal business. Jesse, too."

Cory sighed heavily. "Well, I've got to get to my office." He walked out to his pickup and left without another word.

Judd pondered the situation for a couple minutes before moving it all to the back burner. He mounted his horse and headed for the back ninety.

The morning dragged for Kaitlyn until around noon. Jesse Brandon knocked at the door with the news that her car was ready to be picked up. "Want to ride in to Jackson Hole and get your wheels? You'll need your transportation now that Les is back up and at em."

Although she felt understandably nervous, she grabbed her purse and got in Jesse's dually. Once they were on the highway, Kaitlyn turned toward Jesse as far as her seat belt would let her. "I want you to know how much I appreciate everything you've done for me, Jesse. I know that…that I don't deserve…"

"Whoa, whoa, we've already been there and come back. Now…no more apologies." He glanced at her. "Deal?"

She smiled. "Deal."

After a minute, she asked, "Is it all right if I ask about your wife, Laura? Les told me about the fall she took in the kitchen."

He shot her another glance. She couldn't help but notice the twinkles that exploded in his eyes at the mention of his wife's name.

"She and the baby are just fine—Still waiting for Jesse, Jr. to decide he wants to meet us all." He flashed a smile that matched the sparkles in his eyes and Kaitlyn hated herself for the envy that shot through her insides for Laura Brandon. Not because she had the least feelings for Jesse, but because Laura was loved with such obvious intensity and passion by her man. She hadn't seen anything remotely close to that in her entire life. To be loved just half that much would feel like Heaven had come down. She wanted to meet this woman of Jesse's that was so revered as to invoke a reaction like that from him. How blessed they both were!

It could have easily felt like she'd stepped through some sort of time warp, riding in this truck with Jesse, watching familiar scenes outside the window as they drove down Jackson Hole's main drag. It could have, except her perception of everything around her was so different from when she was here before.

Outwardly, nothing had really changed and she had no particular memories of Jesse that would give her a pause in her emotions. He may have been right about his analysis of what had happened between the two of them. She was a kid looking for a good time, he'd said. Partly, maybe. At least she was glad he remembered her that way. He didn't need the *more* truth of the situation. *Truth* that she was an emotional cripple who couldn't stand alone under the pressure of her family trauma and who had been desperately missing the man she was meant to be with.

It felt like a lifetime ago, that day she had seen the young veterinarian in the barn working on a gimpy little mare with more tenderness than Kaitlyn thought a man could possess. She had watched him all morning and eavesdropped as he whispered and soothed his fidgety patient. She had fantasized a big flowery wedding with this sweet, sexy horse doctor as her groom. That mental picture seemed to have come suddenly out of nowhere and stuck in her imaginings, keeping her awake most of the following night.

Dr. Les Kane. That was his name and he was due to return to the ranch the next morning to work on the mare again. She knew she was *sexying* herself up the next morning because of that fact, but not in a million years would she admit it. Her best fitting jeans, tucked into knee-high cowboy boots and an extra little wiggle as she walked, was meant entirely to make herself feel a little less like a slob, for a change. Wouldn't hurt a bit to clean up a little, she'd decided. Could she help it if the good looking doctor happened to notice?

She just wished she'd been able to handle what she'd started that day instead of causing so much hurt and devastation.

Today, Kaitlyn envisioned herself and all that had happened to her as if being enveloped within a soft and forgiving light. Rehab had taught her how to go there, how to give her pain and anger over into the Hands of a loving Heavenly Father—one day at a time. And that's why she would get her car today and head back to the Double OO with her head held up and find out where life would take her from here. And no matter how it ended, she would be all right.

"How about we get a bite of lunch?" Jesse was already parking head-in to a little diner on main street.

Before he got the door fully open to the diner, an ages old country and western song crooned from an equally old juke box. *Today I, started loving, you, again.* The nostalgia was overwhelming. Kaitlyn's dad was a Merle Haggard fan from her earliest memories and that one song was heard constantly in the barn at the Grace ranch.

But she wasn't thinking about her dad. That song was playing the day she first laid eyes on Les Kane. Her heart swelled at how the lyrics seemed to speak right to her. The only imperfection of the moment was that she was having lunch with the wrong man.

Jesse pointed at a table for two against the far wall. The place was obviously a town favorite. Cowboy hats were dotted around the room, loud talking and laughter almost drowning out old Merle. The dining furniture was something like early pilgrim with a yellow checkered cloth on each table. Kaitlyn loved the place.

Jesse pulled her chair out for her, and then took a seat.

Thirty minutes later, they were finishing the last bites of cheeseburgers and laughing at Jesse's funny dude ranch stories. He was so obviously proud of his family and not in the least ashamed to express it.

She stared at him feeling a tender joy at the true happiness he had found.

He stared back. "What?"

She smiled, eyes twinkling. "I'm so happy for you, Jesse. It's obvious that you've found real honest love." Up to now, they hadn't mentioned each other's private lives.

"Thank you, Kaitlyn. I *am* happy with my life." He hesitated a few seconds. "You know, I've come to believe that there is a certain person that God has already chosen for each of us. And at the right moment, in His time, He'll bring those pairs together. And it'll be a perfect match...Kind of like the way God made Eve from Adam's rib."

"Like you and Laura."

"Like me and Laura, yes. Your perfect mate is on his way to you, too. You just have to wait for it."

She nodded and opened her mouth to reply, but her words were cut off by a man dressed in a three piece suit.

"Well, hello, Jesse Brandon. Hey, how's Laura today. Has your *wife* had that baby yet?"

The man was obnoxious and loud and Kaitlyn recognized the voice immediately. She didn't look at him, but looked down and sipped her tea.

"Not yet." Jesse's tone was short. "Doc, have you met Kaitlyn Grace?"

"We've met." He cut Jesse off causing him to look at Kaitlyn and bringing her head up to look into the accusing glare of Cory Raye. "Surprised to see the two of you in here…together. Small world."

A hot flush rushed into Kaitlyn's face and before she could find her tongue, Cory walked away with a curt, "See ya round," to Jesse.

Jesse had no idea what just happened, but seeing Kaitlyn's embarrassment, he just grinned at her and quipped, "Uh, I don't think that was your rib."

It took a few seconds before it hit, and then she burst out laughing. "Praise the Lord," she managed through her cackles.

Twenty minutes later, she drove her car away from the auto body shop and headed back to Les's.

Jesse sat in his truck a few minutes longer after she left. He let the anger that he had squashed earlier in the diner rise to the surface now that he was alone. He didn't figure it was his business to know what had happened between Kaitlyn and Cory Raye to cause an aversion between them, but he didn't appreciate the public rudeness the man had shown to her. That was uncalled for in any measure. He contemplated a visit to the clinic on his way out of town, and then decided he'd catch the doctor in a more private moment at the ranch.

Right now he needed to get home to Laura.

It was after dark when Les finally got home. He pulled his truck up beside the little black Camry and even though he was exhausted to the bone, a surge of 'yes' galvanized his emotions. He'd been rankled all day long at the words that Cory had assaulted him with that morning about Kaitlyn. He couldn't for the life of him make sense out of it. Had he made a pass at her and didn't take rejection well? Anything was possible while he had moaned and groaned a week of his life away in a sick bed. Well, she was here in *his* cabin and that's all he was going to worry about tonight.

As soon as he opened the front door, he smiled at the intense aroma of garlic and bread. He used the boot jack beside the door, and then padded sock feet into the kitchen.

Kaitlyn looked up to meet his tired, smiling eyes. "Hope you like Italian. My spaghetti is to die for and it's all ready."

"Love it," he replied. "Be right back." He went down the hall to the bathroom and quickly washed up enough to get by until he could shower later. He returned and took his seat at the bar. "A man could get used to this real quick," he said.

"It's just a little supper. No big thing."

"It's a big thing to me. I don't need either one of my hands to count how many times I've come home from work to a hot supper laid out for me. And by a hot chick, no less."

She smiled at him. "I'm glad you think that."

"I'm not *thinking*...I'm *knowing*. I've waited all day just for tonight."

Kaitlyn turned her back to fiddle with a pot on the stove. She knew he wasn't talking about supper and she was torn about how to handle the situation. Her little stint in rehab was beginning to get in her way. In truth, it wasn't rehab. That place had simply shown her how to become a whole person. She had to *accept* what she had learned—that through Jesus Christ was the only way to be whole and the only way to enter Heaven when her time on earth was over. She didn't truly get that for a while, not until she'd had a meltdown in the middle of the night and from her bed at Hope's Ranch, she screamed out *"Jesus, help me"* at the top of her lungs. She had awakened from a tormenting dream that she couldn't even recall the details of afterward. All she remembered was that some distorted looking creature was chasing her while she ran for her life and she remembered that she'd been told by her counselor that *"Jesus will save you if you call to Him."*

When she screamed for His help, an instant calm had enveloped her body and mind. It seemed like Someone had appeared beside her bed suddenly. She knew somehow that if she reached her hand out beside her bed, she would touch that Someone. Then she remembered being told, *"You need to sleep."* The next thing she knew, she was opening her eyes to a bright sunlight filtering through her window.

She knew she had experienced the love of Jesus in person that night. She had spent nearly all of her time afterwards seeking to learn more about this Living God who so dramatically changed her life.

Tonight, standing in Les Kane's kitchen, she knew she was about to be challenged on her commitment to Jesus and His Ways that she'd learned about. In her heart, she had already made the choice.

She sat down and they both dug into the mound of cheesy spaghetti.

"I noticed you've got your car back," Les said between mouthfuls. "Did the shop deliver it out?"

She shook her head. "Jesse took me to town to get it."

Les smiled and nodded, his mouth full of spaghetti. He swallowed and washed it down with a half of a glass of sweet tea. "Jesse Brandon is one fine man. Give you the shirt off his back."

"Yes, I've heard."

She spoke so softly that Les looked up at her. He wondered at the sound of resignation in her tone. "Is something wrong, Katie?"

"No. I'm just a little tired." Actually, she was suddenly feeling sick, both physically and emotionally. Les had to find out about her and Jesse sooner or later. Even though nothing serious had happened between them, just the fact that she had made wedding plans with him on nothing more than a whim, was going to create a breach in everybody's lives out here, including her chances of ever being with Les again.

He smiled. "That's not surprising. You've been jumping through yourself working around here, keeping house and nurse-maiding me for the past week...when you're not busy falling off cliffs and drowning in the mother of all thunderstorms and getting lost in the woods on the darkest night of the year, that is."

He studied her a moment and grew more serious. "We haven't even had fifteen minutes to sit down and have a conversation. I have questions, Katie. But, right now, we're both worn out, so it can wait."

He finished off his tea, swiveled the barstool around and got up. "You did not lie, Miss Grace." He patted his bronc-rider flat belly and winked at her. "That *was* to die for. I'm headed for a hot, soapy shower. Want to join me?" He shifted his eyebrows up and down in a teasing gesture.

She knew this was coming, and *yes,* she wanted to. She wanted to more than jump in the shower with him. She wanted to jump his gorgeous bones. It's not like they hadn't already been there with each other before. God, they had already made a baby together. That little baby boy was the only good and perfect thing that had ever come to her life.

But too many had been hurt by her wrong doing, even her baby. Jesus had forgiven her and gave her another chance to do things right. The hard part was forgiving herself. But she couldn't—wouldn't deliberately allow herself to hurt her Savior. That's where the rubber meets the road. WWJD? When faced with a hard decision, that's the question she chose to ask to get her answer. What Would Jesus Do? She knew the answer and tonight, almost wished she didn't.

"I...I'll wait until you're done. I'll do dishes while you shower," she answered without looking at him.

He stood a minute, and then left the kitchen without another word. She knew he had no clue that she was dying inside to follow him down the hall. Her body and mind was screeching at her to go with him, but something else was holding her feet to the floor. Or so it seemed.

She forced herself to clean up the supper mess. She got the worst of it done before she sat down. Trembling and unnaturally exhausted, she felt a little nauseous. Too much stress. She knew the sooner she got her secrets out in the open with Les, told him everything, the sooner she would be able to truly move forward with her life. She knew he was going to hate her after he found out, but she needed to tell him. Now. Later would only make the results harder to bear. She didn't really believe that, though. The thought of losing him again was killing her soul.

But that was the new plan. Tonight she would tell him the whole story and leave for Missouri in the morning.

Besides, if she stayed much longer, she was going to wind up in Les's bed and shower and anywhere else he wanted her to go with him. As much as she wanted to do things right, she knew she was going to lose this battle if she stayed any longer.

When she got up, her head spun with dizziness, her legs weak, like weights were wrapped around her ankles. Then she grabbed her stomach and moaned when her insides felt like they flipped upside down.

Les entered the kitchen in time to hear her moan and see her face turn pale. He took her arm to steady her and reached behind him almost in the same instant to grab a tall, plastic trash can. He held it under her face in the nick of time, then set it on the floor and held her steady until she was through. Her entire body heaved and trembled.

"Hold the sides of this can and don't move," he instructed, and then he dashed to the bathroom to wet a clean washcloth.

She was embarrassed at this whole incident. Of all the gross things she could have done, this had to be the worst. Holding somebody while they puked up spaghetti was disgusting. Oh geez, she felt so sick and unhinged at the same time.

She tried to shut down the next thought that popped into her head, but, *Les will gag at the idea of ever kissing me again,* shot through her mind before she could stop it. Of all places for her mind to go right now!

Les held on to her and walked her to the bathroom. He continued to hold her while she washed her mouth and teeth, then handed her a fresh, cold, wet cloth to bathe her face. Rather than walk her to the bedroom, he scooped her up into his arms and carried her there.

"I'm sorry, Les."

"Really? I bet you're not sorry at all." He laid her shaky body on the cool sheets. "In fact, I bet your little heart's doing the happy dance right now after the week you just spent taking care of my puny butt." He bent down and kissed her forehead. When he pulled back, his eyes were big and the humor gone from them. He laid his hands on either side of her neck, then felt of her arms. "You've got fever. I'll be right back," he said, then left.

Within a minute he was back with the same bottle of fever reducer she had fed him the week before and a cup of water. He slipped his hand under the back of her neck and lifted her enough to drink.

"Looks like you caught my flu bug. But just to be safe, you've got to see a doctor."

Kaitlyn closed her eyes and tried to will herself to be well. Most likely, Les would call for Cory and that disgusted her as much as puking up spaghetti.

Les was thinking hard. He had two ways to go. He could drive her in to Jackson's hospital ER or ask Cory to come out here. And nothing, with the exception of an emergency, would allow him to call Cory.

He didn't give her a choice, but got her up and helped her to his dually. She curled up on the seat and rested her head on a pillow that he tucked partly in his lap. He caressed her hair, smoothing it back from the side of her face, and then rested his arm along her side, his fingers splayed across her hip. He said little during the ride to the hospital.

His thoughts were another story. He thought it odd how natural he felt taking care of this woman—like she was his to take care of, for better or worse. He would protect her with his life, if need be, even from butt-heads like Cory Raye.

Then, on the other hand was the truth of the matter. Kaitlyn was *not* his. She showed up here out of the clear blue—or the black of a stormy night. He'd never gotten a chance to ask her why she was here. Maybe she was only passing through, like she said, and this was all a coincidence. He had no answers to that, but one thing he did know. He wanted this woman—for better or worse.

Kaitlyn had never been so sick in her life. Waves of nausea caused a moan to escape from her throat now and then. The only bit of comfort came from Les's occasional pat on her hip and leg.

Nearly three hours later, she was back in Les's bed. The ER doctor diagnosed the flu, gave her two hypo's in her hip and a bottle of antibiotic capsules. Doctor's orders were to stay in bed and drink fluids. No problem staying in bed. She couldn't move her big toe without being nauseated. *Thank you, Lord, for directing my steps today.* Not funny, she mused.

That was her last thought before sinking into a deep solid sleep.

***

CHAPTER SEVEN

Les moved quietly and methodically as he saddled Billy Joe, one of the ranch's working horses. The big bay gelding was his favorite and was left alone by the other hands. Each cowboy picked his mount and generally considered it his own during work days.

He had left Kaitlyn only after getting her first pill down her for the day. A couple of sips of sprite were all she could handle. After having been there himself, he hated trying to force her to so much as raise her head. But he planned to check on her by noon.

"Hey, Mister Les, guess what?"

Les turned toward the familiar little girl he had grown to love. He knew Judd would be only a step behind his daughter.

"Morning, Les." Judd spoke as he stepped into the breezeway of the barn.

"Morning." Les responded to Abigail's bear hug around his hips with a pat on her back. Abby Luke was always quick with a hug for Les no matter where she encountered him and of course, melted him every time. This morning she was dressed like a wrangler about to saddle up for work.

"Hey squirt, aren't you supposed to be on a school bus about now?" He tugged on her ponytail.

She giggled as only Abby could. "No, silly. I don't go to school yet."

"Well, silly me." Les chuckled at her, and then realized, school or not, it was Saturday.

Toni, the wife and mom of the crew entered the barn carrying a thermos mug of coffee with steam rising out of the drinking slit in the top of the lid.

"Hey there, Les." Her smile was quick and contagious.

"Toni," he responded, grinning. "You ladies are out early this morning."

"Yep. We get to play cowgirls today," Toni answered.

Toni Luke was known for being a top hand with a horse. Raised by her Uncle on a small ranch in Texas, she had learned the old school ways of roping and riding. But she also had a remarkable way with a fresh or unruly horse. Something she'd learned from her Uncle John Baxter that he had not shared with anyone except her. Some called it *horse whispering*. Toni didn't talk about it. If you questioned her, she'd just smile and leave it at that. But it seemed to be a fail-proof method. It was only recently that she had started seriously riding again. Judd's and Toni's life seemed to revolve around their daughter's well-being and their church ministry held in their home.

Having watched this little family's interaction with each other over the past years, Les couldn't help but admire their genuineness. And neither could he help but feel a twinge of envy at the purity of their love that he couldn't really relate to and never expected to have in his life's experience. He didn't attend their church meetings and they never preached at him about anything. They just lived by their convictions rather than talk about it much.

Judd now had three horses tethered in the alley. Toni stepped inside the tack room to begin saddling up, instructing Abby where to stand out of danger.

Judd walked around in front of Les and apologetically offered his hand in a proper greeting for his ranch foreman. "I'm certainly glad to see you back to yourself. You had us a little worried."

"Thanks. I'm good to go. But I guess Kaitlyn picked up the bug. She's in bed now with the same symptoms."

Judd was taken aback for a moment. "Does she need to see a doctor?"

"I took her to the ER in Jackson last night. It hit her suddenly like it did me. She's got the same meds I had."

Judd looked down for a moment, not sure how to brooch the subject of Kaitlyn with Les. "So...are these all coincidences that's keeping her at the cabin with you? Or is there more to you and this young lady than that?"

Les wasn't prepared for that type of question and it produced a churning of emotions in him. His reaction was enough answer for Judd to get the idea, but he refused to assume anything. Judd required spoken words for answers when he asked questions. Assuming usually produced trouble. So he waited while Les searched for his reply.

"There's more," he said evenly. Les knew the rules about overnight female guests in the bunkhouse and in the foreman's quarters. Judd was a stickler about that and knew that's what prompted his question. So he added, "But coincidences *have* kept her from leaving up to now."

Judd nodded. "Okay. If you want to talk about it, you know I'm always available."

"Thanks. I'll keep that in mind."

"Is there anything Toni or I can do to help with Kaitlyn's flu bug?"

"Might be a good idea to steer clear of my place for now. I can take care of her myself. You don't want your family exposed any more than they already are. That's one bad bug."

"Daddy, come on. We're burning daylight."

Both men looked at the little girl already sitting on her pony and laughed.

"I'm coming." Judd joined his family where Toni was holding his saddled horse.

Les mounted up and rode out of the barn.

The morning's work was hard for Les to get through. Over the past few years, he had dug post holes, strung barbed wire and branded cowhide until he could smell the sizzling hair just by thinking about it. His riding ability had improved until he felt more comfortable in the saddle than he did standing on the ground. He worked, he ate, he slept. He had forced his mind onto the job at hand while the months and years passed by.

Today, he couldn't quite get there no matter how busy he was or how much activity was going on around him. For the first time since he'd arrived at the Double OO Ranch and hired on, something felt out of kilter. The contentment of his emotionally drab days was suddenly gone. He had to force every move he made and kept mainly to himself.

He was concerned about Kaitlyn being so sick. He was worried about how he was going to continue on day-to-day if she left and went home. He'd been in love with her since the moment he'd first seen her. How on earth had he been able to function for so long a time? Because today, she was all he could think about. It was like a Rip Van Winkle awakening. He wasn't satisfied with sleeping his days away—to just *exist* anymore.

Change was in the air. He could smell it. But change can come in many flavors and not always to the liking.

Billy Joe was tired and needed a break, so Les let him walk back rather than push him to hurry, even though it was well after noon. He scanned the countryside with a growing melancholy that he would not be viewing this place in this same way for much longer. He was familiar with every square foot of this ranch and had made a few good friends. But he believed every beginning also had an ending—of some sort.

Arriving home, he dismounted and tied Billy Joe to a low tree limb close to the house. He'd locked the cabin when he left that morning. He retrieved his extra key from inside the light globe beside the door where he had hidden it when he first moved in. When he pushed it into the keyhole, the door opened. Not only was it unlocked, but not fully closed. He knew it was locked when he left that morning. He'd double checked it. Kaitlyn must have opened it and not closed it back right.

When he got to the bedroom, it didn't appear that she had moved a muscle in hours. A heavy quilt was pulled up to half cover her face. When he laid his hand on the side of her face, she moaned and flickered her eyelids.

Les squatted beside the bed, mindful of the spurs sticking up on the end of his boot heels and hunkered close to look into her face. "Hey, little lady," his voice low and gravelly. He caressed her cheek with the back of his hand and felt the heat of her fever, then pulled the quilt off of her face.

She opened her eyes. "Hi. Why did you change your hat?"

Les grinned at her obvious sleepy fevered remark. "Oh, you know me. I'm a man of many hats. Are you hungry?"

"No," she croaked.

"Yeah, I know. But you *have* to try to swallow something. Have you been out of bed to… the bathroom?"

"Don't need to."

He stood. "Okay. I'll be right back." He'd question her later when she was more awake.

Minutes later, Les carried her medicine along with a cup of hot chicken broth and a glass of water to her bedside. He set the tray down and helped her sit up as he stuffed a pillow behind her.

"I'm so knocked out, Les. Just let me sleep."

"You got something to help you sleep in one of those hypos last night. Let's get these pills down and see if you can drink some broth."

She managed the pills and sip of water, then slid down under the cover and went back out.

Les understood how she felt, but knew he'd have to get the broth in her by supper time.

Feeling his own hunger raging he went to the kitchen and loaded a Jethro-sized sandwich and large glass of ice water. One of the two oversized white rocking chairs that decorated the wrap around porch out back beckoned. He took a monster bite of sandwich as he headed toward the back door, but stopped chewing suddenly and stared. A white ball cap was lying on the floor by the door. He picked it up and read the logo, High Point Dude Ranch, printed on the front with the name Jesse written in smaller letters on the cap's bill. These hats were given out as advertisement at High Point. He had one himself, except his was blue. Jesse always joked that he was the only one who got to wear the white hat on his ranch. Plus, the inside hat band was sweat stained.

Les turned the hat over in his hands and looked up at the back door that he'd found open when he got home. Was Jesse here? Did Kaitlyn get up and open the door for him? Maybe he needed a vet.

He finished his sandwich where he was standing, went out and locked the door behind him. With the ball cap stuck inside his shirt, he rode Billy Joe to the barn, unsaddled and put him in his stall with a block of fresh grass hay. He fished his truck key out of his jeans pocket and drove the few miles to Jesse's ranch. The place looked deserted, but he knew business had been shut down for a few weeks.

He tried the barn first, but no one was there. Then it dawned that Laura might be in the hospital. He headed for the back door of the house when he heard Jesse's voice.

"In here, Les."

He stepped around a seven foot high cedar plank privacy wall onto a covered concrete patio complete with a hot tub and several chairs and table sets with big red umbrellas. The huge pots of fake cactus and real flowering fall colored hanging baskets were eye popping, to say the least.

Jesse and Laura were sitting at a table drinking coffee and sharing a newspaper. Les looked from one to the other and grinned. "Well, if you two don't take the cake. How's it going with the baby?"

"Come in here and have a seat, Les. We're all fine. Laura's checking into the hospital late this evening. Gonna induce this one in the morning."

Les pulled out a chair and sat down. "Well, I certainly hope it all happens quickly for you, Laura."

"Thank you. Want something to drink?"

"No thanks." He pulled the cap out of his shirt and handed it to Jesse.

Jesse gave a surprised half grin at Les. "Where did you come up with this? I've hunted high and low for this thing."

"Were you at my place this morning looking for me?" Les asked, expecting his question to ring a bell.

"No." Jesse shook his head, not missing the confusion that darted through Les's eyes.

"I picked it up off my kitchen floor a few minutes ago. Are you sure you…"

"Positive. Last time I wore it was yesterday afternoon." He squinted his eyes in thought. "Actually, I remember taking it off in the barn. Sweat was running in my eyes and I took it off to swipe my arm across my face. I figured I laid it down, but never could find it again. He looked at Les then as if it just registered what he'd said. "Your kitchen floor?" He examined the hat to be sure it was his. Then he settled a strange look on Laura and she widened her eyes and shook her head.

"Don't look at me. I don't wear your stinky hats. And do I *look* like I could have gone five miles to throw your hat in Les Kane's kitchen floor? I can't even get out of this chair without help!"

Les lowered his head and choked back a laugh.

"Pregnant woman alert!" Jesse announced good naturedly.

"Very pregnant woman alert," Laura corrected, eyes twinkling .

Les got up. "I better get back. Kaitlyn's in bed with the flu now. She's too sick to be left alone very long."

"Is there anything we can do for you or Kaitlyn before we leave for the hospital this evening?" Jesse asked with all sincerity.

"Would you like for me to go stay with her this afternoon?" Hank and Martha have the kids. I'm available and I would love to meet her." Laura offered enthusiastically.

"Un-be-lievable," was all Les could say as he stared at them like they'd just sprouted angel wings. "Thanks, but I've got it in hand. This flu is highly contagious. I'm keeping everybody away for a few days. You two just get that baby here." Les met Jesse's gaze and held it long enough to send the message to *follow me.*

Jesse walked him to his truck that was parked at the barn.

"I'm not sure, but I think someone may have used my extra key and come in the back door while I was out. I definitely locked the door when I left and it was unlocked and left part way open. Your cap was on the floor just inside. Judd and his family were out on the range with me all morning. No one, except Judd, knows about that key."

"What about Kaitlyn? Did she hear any noises?"

"I'm not sure. She's been too knocked out from her meds. I don't think she had moved a muscle all morning. I barely got her awake enough to swallow her pills when I came in around lunch time."

Jesse was thinking hard, trying to make rhyme or reason out of his cap. How? Who?

"Look, Jesse, I just wanted you to know this, but for now, take care of your business here. I'll keep a closer eye out at home, at least while Katie is sick."

Jesse nodded and Les loaded up and drove out. Jesse stood there an extra minute, not contemplating the mystery surrounding his cap, but the soft inflection when Les said *Katie.* He looked down at the ground and grinned. He truly hoped this turned out to be a good thing for the two of them.

Jesse Dane, Jr. chose to arrive that night at midnight after thirty minutes of labor. Laura was up running around like nothing had happened the next morning, ready to get the Brandon bunch all home and on a schedule.

Jesse never ceased his amazement at his once citified little wife, now as hard country as a string bean. Nothing ever seemed to ruffle her feathers much. She just rolled with the flow of his cowboy life, both of her feet in the thick of it all. Two kids didn't slow her down and it didn't appear three would either.

Hank and Martha Walton were God sent for more reasons than one. Having no other family that anyone knew about, the aging pair took the position of Gramps and Granny. They worked tirelessly cooking and cleaning for the dude ranch guests and took care of Andy and Anna Leigh when they were needed—and when they weren't needed.

From the day, a couple of years ago, when God had shown up in his barn in the form of a very supernatural miracle, that caused his beloved dying horse to stand up healed and whole in an instant, Jesse's heart was broken and humbled before his Lord. He never let the sun rise or set over his house without giving thanks on bended knees for the blessings God lavished on him. Once, Andy had walked into an empty stall in the barn where Jesse was offering his evening praise and caught him on his knees. Andy backed out and never mentioned it. But, not long afterward, Jesse saw Andy through the crack in his bedroom door, on his knees and head bowed. His daddy heart swelled and burst, dripping more thanks down his face.

As he walked out of the hospital that afternoon carrying his new baby son and namesake in his arms, praise to his God filled his heart once more.

Les didn't want to put names out there to Jesse. The time wasn't right anyway with the baby coming and all. But something was amiss with Cory Raye. Their encounter at the fence line was bugging him, especially now. Seemed to Les like a good place to start asking questions.

First thing tomorrow morning, he would take a little trip to the medical clinic in Jackson Hole. Then it hit him that tomorrow was Sunday. Maybe he'd have to catch him after church services at the Luke home. Les didn't attend, but he knew Cory did.

At home, he found Kaitlyn at least half awake. He felt of her forehead, hoping it was cooler by now, but she was still too warm.

"Hey," he spoke as tenderly as he might have to a small child. "How are you feeling?"

"Like poo," she whimpered.

He chuckled. "Yep, I remember that feeling. I've got a deal for you. How about you go get a shower while I change your bed sheets and get you something to eat?"

"That's not necessary. I can take care of my sheets and I'm not hungry."

"One of those kind, huh. Yeah, well, okay, let's get you headed toward the shower." He helped her sit up on the side of the bed. "There you go."

She stood up, shocked at how wobbly her legs felt. Every muscle in her body felt raw.

Les knew what she was going through. He'd been there, done that. "Just head for the shower. I'll put some clean clothes in there for you."

As soon as he heard her close the shower door, he hung one of his longest T-shirts and her undies from her suitcase on the towel racks. He left the bathroom door cracked open enough so he could hear her.

Quickly, he stripped the bed and put the extra set of clean sheets on. He filled the washing machine with the used sheets and snatched the clothes she had dropped on the floor of the bathroom, to top off the load.

Chicken noodle soup was heating in the microwave and he managed to fix her tray about the same time she opened the door and headed back to bed.

By the time she had showered and washed her hair, she felt a little better. As soon as she propped herself up on the pillows Les had fluffed up for her, he appeared with a supper tray.

""Here you are, young lady. Hot chicken soup, the cure for whatever ails you." He set the tray on the bedside table and tried to hand her a large, half-filled mug.

Nothing about the idea of swallowing food or drink was appealing. In fact, she just couldn't do it. "I can't. I can't swallow anything."

He stood there, mug in hand, and took another stab at it. "Here's the deal. Either you take a few sips of this broth or I'm hauling you back to the ER and let them poke you in the butt with another needle. What's it gonna be?"

After a few seconds, "If I swallow that, I'll throw up. Wait til tomorrow. I'll eat tomorrow."

Boy, did he ever remember that feeling. "All right," he conceded. "Tomorrow for sure?"

"Yes."

He set the mug down and took out the extra pillows, leaving one for her head. Then he tucked her in and left her alone.

An hour later, the laundry was in the dryer and the kitchen back in order.

Remembering he'd left some mail in his truck days ago, he went out and gathered up several envelopes of one sort or another. One more was peeking out from under the front seat. He reached and pulled out a small red notebook. He didn't remember seeing it before. He opened the front cover and realized immediately it was Kaitlyn's. It looked sort of like a diary and not one to trespass on another's privacy, he closed the cover. But, not before his eyes had skimmed the first page. What he had read registered only after he had closed it.

He opened the front cover again and written in Kaitlyn's handwriting was *Hope's Rehabilitation Ranch, where I met Jesus and was raised from the dead.*

"What in the…" Les was not in favor of snooping in another person's private affairs, but it was going to happen this time. He felt like this book held the answers to questions he hadn't been able to ask Katie since she showed up here.

He thumbed through pages of one-sentence notes and scriptures that were written in all directions on the pages. Things like *Jesus Loves Kaitlyn Grace. Jesus Died For Kaitlyn Grace. All of Kaitlyn's Sins Are Now Forgiven. God Is Love. God Is Good All Of The Time.*

Another page had, *Father God, Thank You For Ordering My Steps Today,* written big to fill up the whole page.

On another page was a scripture with a note in parenthesis, *(Memorize this today).* It said, *John 3:16 For God so loved the world, that He gave His only begotten Son, that whosoever believeth in Him should not perish, but have Everlasting Life.*

Near the end of the book was a page that said, *"To be absent from the body, is to be present with the Lord. II Corinthians 5:8.*

Les knew some of this was scriptures from the Bible, but he had no idea what any of it really meant. He hadn't learned what he expected to—until he got to the last page. It was entitled: *People I Must Forgive and Ask Forgiveness Of.* Her parents and brother, Wade, were listed first. Then a child, he assumed, called baby Dan. Then his own name under that. *Les.*

But it was the next and final name on the list that grabbed his belly into a knot. *Jesse Brandon.*

Why was Jesse's name on this list? It had to have been written there before the night of her accident, because the book had been under this truck seat ever since then. He sat in stunned and confused silence for a long time. What was he missing here? Did Katie know Jesse before she came on this trip? But, how?

His mind darted back to the night he had brought Kaitlyn home with him. He had gone into Jesse's house to see if Laura was all right and Jesse had asked him if Kaitlyn was a friend or family member of his. He remembered Jesse acting a little odd, like he had something more to say, but didn't. Not in all of this time has he let on that *he* knew who she was.

So this was why she came to Wyoming—at least, one of the reasons—to clear her conscience. She *had* come here to see him, after all. But why Jesse?

***

CHAPTER EIGHT

Les numbly gathered up his mail along with Kaitlyn's journal and took it in to the house. He shoved it all into a kitchen drawer where he kept his mail and various papers.

Checking on Katie would normally be his next move, but instead, he headed back out, got in his truck and went to Jackson Hole.

He felt like a silent, but deafening blow had landed in the middle of his heart. Instead of assuming, he knew he should stop the churning in his mind and wait for the facts. Cory's verbal attack on Katie was disgusting in itself, but add in that little red book with Jesse's name on a list of people from her past and confusion and turmoil would naturally take over. And he'd gone as long as he intended to without getting some answers.

Kaitlyn was too sick. He wouldn't confront her while she was in that state. And most likely there wasn't any confrontation to it. This should turn out to be simple and inconsequential.

So, she had spent time in a rehab facility. Obviously, a church type of rehab. That certainly wasn't a bad thing. And he had noticed a change in her since she'd been here. She was emotionally stronger, more self-assured than she was a few years ago. He'd loved her the way she used to be and he loved her now. He couldn't conceive of learning anything about Kaitlyn that was going to change his mind about that.

Jackson Hole was gearing up for its usual Saturday night rush of tourists and local partiers. He knew Cory's clinic would be closed, but he had a good idea where to look for him.

He parked a block from a popular downtown bar and grille, which was walking distance from Cory's condo. Inside the eatery, he spotted him perched on a barstool with his supper in front of him. Les straddled the stool beside him.

With a bottle of beer raised to his lips, Cory twisted around to see who had joined him. He took a swig. "Hello there, Les. What brings you to town tonight?"

Les ordered a beer before he said anything. Then, "I want to talk to you about your remarks about Kaitlyn."

"Well, don't beat around the bush. Get right to the point." Cory good naturedly slapped Les's shoulder, chuckling like he'd just won a bet.

Les felt his whole head heat up. "All right. Either you owe that young *lady* a huge apology or you owe *me* a damn good explanation."

Cory rolled his empty beer bottle in a circle between his hands and stared at it intently for nearly a minute.

Les looked at him and waited, holding his own full bottle of beer in a death grip.

Finally, Cory swiveled his stool around to face his angry friend. "I apologize to *you* for offending you. I didn't know you and…that girl…were actually an item."

"That girl has a name. It's Kaitlyn. She's the one you offended, even if it was behind her back. Not me."

"Look, Les, that girl…Kaitlyn, isn't who you think she is. She's not a stranger around here who had some bad luck a long way from home."

Les stiffened and sat back suddenly. A flash of *Jesse Brandon* written in her book shot through his inner vision. "What are you talking about?" Les's eyes were boring holes through Cory's.

"Don't you remember awhile back when Jesse's fiancé ditched him…Ran off without a word?"

Les blinked. "I heard something about it. I hadn't been around here very long…Didn't know either of them. What's that got to do with Kaitlyn?"

Cory's eyes flashed with out-of-place laughter. "She was the little runaway bride-to-be."

It took a few seconds to register those words, and then Les leaped off of his barstool, his fists clenched. More than anything else he could think of, he wanted to knock Cory Raye's teeth down his throat. Not because of the absurdity of his statement, but because he already knew there was or had, obviously, been something between Katie and Jesse. But not that! It *couldn't* have been that.

"That's a rotten lie, Raye. That's not even a possibility." Les raised his voice enough to turn a few cowboy-hatted heads toward him and bring the bartender over with a warning glare.

"Why don't you go home and ask her? Ask her how she got from High Point Dude Ranch to the Jackson airport the day she ran off. She and Jesse were supposed to be married in a few days, so I learned later."

"Later...from what?"

"She paid me one hundred dollars to drive her to the airport. I didn't have a clue who she was, then. But I gave her back her money when I saw her at Judd's barn a couple days ago. Found out after the fact what I'd helped her do to Jesse...Broke his heart."

Shocked confusion only mildly described what was running through Les's veins at that moment. He wanted to believe Cory was mistaking Kaitlyn for some other woman. He thought hard to place the timing for all this. He vaguely remembered hearing some talk among the Double OO hands about Jesse Brandon's woman disappearing without a word. They joked about being glad they were working for the Double OO and not High Point and steering clear of Jesse until his wound at least grew a scab.

He didn't know Jesse at that time. He'd never met him. He was too busy trying to grow a scab over his own heart and stayed hid out as far back as the ranch boundaries would allow.

If the woman *was* Kaitlyn, Les surmised, she would have been here romancing Jesse at the same time he was out here working. No. It didn't add up. But then, why was Jesse's name on Kaitlyn's list in her journal—before she even got here. And his vest pocket still had the hundred dollar bill in it that Judd thought might be hers. He pulled it out and let it fly into the front of Cory's shirt.

Without another word, he turned, walked out, got in his truck and drove slowly back toward home. Cory's last words, *'Broke his heart'* ran over and over through his head. He felt sick to his stomach. He didn't want to go back to his cabin tonight. Turmoil and grief and anger were all beating him over the head at once.

He wanted to go straight to High Point and get the story from Jesse. But he'd just gotten Laura home with a new baby. He wouldn't upset Laura. Not tonight. And Kaitlyn was too sick to go there with, which was the very reason he *had* to go home tonight. He couldn't leave her alone in that condition.

How he was going to be able to handle himself around her, he couldn't say. His emotions ran from pain to anger to disbelief—all wrapped up in confusion.

When in God's name did she have time to meet Jesse, fall in love and plan a wedding? Fall in love. Fall in love. He squeezed his eyes shut on a swell of pain. When he opened them, tears spilled over onto his cheeks.

The house was dark and quiet when he finally went inside. Unless she had been up to the bathroom, she hadn't been up at all, which said, she wasn't feeling any better.

He peeked into the dark bedroom, her slow, even breathing telling him she was asleep.

He had pulled himself together before he came in the house and went about getting her pills and a light supper together. He was almost glad she was unable to talk about this right now, because he was too emotionally charged to trust himself to not do something he might later regret.

He turned her lamp on and set the tray down. "Kaitlyn?" He didn't touch her and fought to hold a rein on his temper.

She slowly opened her eyes and stared up into his face. "Hi. What time is it?"

"Eight o'clock." He was having a hard time pretending everything was the same as when he'd seen her earlier that day. "Your medicine is on this tray...Some soup and a sandwich...A glass of sprite. Do the best you can with it." He stepped back, intending to turn and leave.

"Les?" She'd heard the flat stoniness in his voice.

He stopped. "Yeah?"

"Is...something wrong?"

He stood, undecided a moment. Looking at her fevered eyes, he knew this wasn't the time. "Ranch business," he lied. "I'll be out most of the night. Try to eat and take those pills." He turned and left.

Once again, he was behind the wheel of his truck, but had no idea where he was going to spend the night. He *did* know it wouldn't be in the house with her. He wasn't feeling particularly broken hearted. He was too angry for that. And as far as he was concerned, he didn't care if he stayed that way the rest of his life. Anger was easier to bear. He had hurt over that woman in there with guilty pain, self- abasing pain, until he was sure it had sapped extra years off of his life. She wasn't getting another moment of that waste of time.

He backed out and drove away, contemplating a bed of hay in the barn. But come morning, he'd be faced with questions from somebody, so that that out. The bunkhouse was not an option. He headed for Jackson Hole. A motel bed would suit his weary bones just fine.

Kaitlyn heard the truck leave. She knew something more than ranch business was wrong with Les. He was mad at something or someone and it had been silently spewed all over her. Les had spoken to her and looked at her with nothing but disgust. She knew. He had to have heard about her and Jesse.

Her stomach twisted into a knot. Why hadn't she told him herself? Whatever someone else had told him, it couldn't be the entire truth. No one knew that, except her.

She wanted to dress and go after him. Drive until she found his pickup and tell him everything tonight. But when she sat up on the side of the bed, her head swam. Her legs were so weak and trebly that just walking to the bathroom and back exhausted her.

"Oh, Les," she whispered, forcing herself to sit on the side of the bed. "Oh, Jesus," she whispered and dissolved into sobs.

Her head began pounding. She forced herself to stop crying and swallow her prescription pills along with the pain meds Les had left on her bedside table. It took her most of ten minutes to swallow about half of the soup and sandwich. She didn't want to eat, but knew she had to help herself get well. Her life was falling to pieces and she could hardly get her head off the pillow to try to salvage it. If that was even possible. She lay back down and cried herself to sleep.

It was just after sunup when she opened her eyes. The memory of the past evening flooded her mind and she felt a resurgence of pain squeezing her guts. Had Les even come home last night?

The tray set on the bedside table, except it had a fresh plate of scrambled eggs and toast on it, along with more pills. A glass of water and cup of lukewarm coffee was there, too.

Hope sprang into her heart, bringing her easily to her feet. A slow walk through the house proved she was alone. The couch hadn't been slept on, but he had definitely come in to take care of her this morning.

In passing, she noticed the kitchen was a class A disaster, but she was glad about that. She would force herself to dress and look alive and clean up his mess. Maybe he wasn't so angry today and they could finally talk.

She ate most of the cold breakfast, took her pills and showered. Jeans rolled to her calves and a short sleeved pale yellow T-shirt at least made her look better. She had to rest a while before forcing her way to the kitchen.

Les was in and out of the cabin in a good hour before the sun peeked through the trees. He'd already been to the barn and rode Billy Joe to the house, leaving him tied to a tree limb while he fixed a tray for Kaitlyn.

He struggled to close his mind to images of her and Jesse together. He needed to help her get well and get her out of his house and his life once and for all. This time, he could move on. His heart would never be at a woman's mercy again. It had stolen years from him, learning this, but it was a lesson *well* learned. From here on out, he'd live by his own rules and keep his heart to himself.

Les rousted out the crew way before dawn amidst more grumbling than he'd ever heard from them. But he wasn't in the mood for it, so he just shouted his instructions at them and left.

They had a fire burning by daybreak, preparing to do some fall branding. Les worked like a madman all morning. He rode hard, roped hard, whooped louder and laughed longer at the men's half-hearted jokes. He was on overkill with every move he made until Judd rode up beside Billy Joe and called a halt to his madness.

"Let's take a break, Les."

Les jerked his head toward his boss as if he was seeing an apparition. He hadn't noticed Judd out all day and the scowl on his face didn't look like this was going to bode well for him. Both men stopped their horses.

"Problem, boss?"

"Looks that way." Judd prayed himself calm. "I need you to go tell the boys that work is over for the day. I'll wait for you."

Les blinked at him, and then looked out across the valley at the spread of cowboys, horses and calves. He sucked a deep breath, his first easy lung full of air all day. He lifted his battered and stained Stetson and raked his splayed fingers through his hair before he settled it back on and bumped Billy Joe into a trot. At that moment, he remembered. It was Sunday.

He had rousted these cowboys out before dawn to work on their day off. Some of them always attended cowboy church services at Judd's home. No wonder the boss was in a wad.

Les had pulled some stupid stunts in his time, but this one would top his list. After instructing the hands to go on home, he rode back to Judd who was eyeing him with that usual contemplative expression that he wore a lot. The two men sat side by side on their horses for a few minutes without a word spoken.

Finally, "Wanna tell me what this is all about, Les?"

Oddly enough, he *did* want to talk to somebody. Unflinching, he nodded.

Judd led the way farther into the valley and both men dismounted beside a still flaming branding fire. He waved off the lone cowboy who was trotting over to douse the fire. "Leave it, Rowdy." Judd shouted. The man raised his gloved hand, turned his horse around and loped toward the barn.

The wind was picking up and coming in with a chill. Both men settled on a couple of small boulder-like rocks beside the fire pit that had been dragged there years ago by a couple of industrious Double OO hands.

There was that pensive look again on Judd as he studied Les's face for several seconds. "Tough day?"

Les clasped his fingers together between his spread knees. He hung his head feeling like something that had just crawled out from under the rock he was sitting on. "Something like that. I'm sorry about today, Judd. Guess I lost track of my days, somehow."

"Got anything to do with the young lady staying with you?"

Les nodded. "Yes sir, but she'll be leaving in a day or two... as soon as she's well enough to drive. That'll be the end of that." He was struggling to hold on to his anger. Anything less would cause him to crumble in front of the ranch boss. One more screw-up and he'd have to leave the state to save face.

Judd knew there was more to Les and Kaitlyn than this cowboy was giving up. He knew well how a woman could turn a man's guts inside out and he knew what he was witnessing on Les, no matter how hard he was trying to hide it. He gave him a sidelong glance, and asked, "I'm just wondering, what kind of a foreman am I going to be left with after Miss Grace is gone?"

Les squeezed his eyes shut and swallowed hard.

Judd nodded his head up and down. Les's reaction had answered his question. "That's what I figured. So I'm supposing this is a one way street? She doesn't have the same feelings for you?"

"Yeah, she thinks she does, but..." He paused, not sure how much *gut spilling* he wanted to do.

"But?" Judd figured Les must have heard some gossip about Miss Grace and he hoped he'd talk about it. This kind of festering pain could prove to damage more than just his love life.

"Don't worry about my job here suffering. I haven't let you down yet, have I? Except for today, that is."

"That's just a beginning, Les, and she's not gone yet."

"I came here three or so years ago to work her out of my mind and I haven't..." He blurted that out before he thought.

Judd blinked and sat up straighter, his frown deepening. "I see. So, this isn't new. Is she an ex-wife? Ex-girlfriend?"

"Fiancé. We were engaged a few years ago."

Whew! For the first time, Judd began to wonder about Kaitlyn Grace's character. Especially if what he'd heard about her and Jesse was true. "If you want to unload, I'm good for that."

Les let out a long, slow breath, then, unloaded. From the day he'd met Kaitlyn, to causing the death of Mae-Belle, to his talk with Cory Raye yesterday, it all poured out. "A woman who can hop from one man to another like that can't be trusted. I don't know why she was at High Point three years ago. I was working here and didn't have a clue she was even in Wyoming."

"Have you talked to Jesse about this?"

Les shook his head and bit at his bottom lip. "I only heard about it yesterday. He's got that new baby and all. And there's Laura."

Something was pinging in Judd's spirit, but he didn't understand it yet. There seemed to be more to this whole deal than was showing on the surface. "Well, I've got to hand it to you, Les. Most men would have barged in on those people lives without a thought. You've got a good heart...Selfless."

Les's mouth lifted sardonically. "I wouldn't go that far. I spent last night in Jackson Hole to keep from doing something stupid."

"That's what I mean."

The two men's eyes met for the first time across the small camp fire and Judd saw something he'd never witnessed on his ranch foreman until now. Fear. And he knew what had been moving inside of him a few minutes ago. The Spirit of God was all over the young veterinarian, dealing with his soul. *Use me however you need to, Lord.*

"I don't know, Judd. Maybe it's time I moved on. As much as I love this job and all, I don't know that I can go on like nothing's changed."

"Well, now, let's don't get hasty with packing it in. If it turns out that God is moving you on, then I'll help you pack up."

Les frowned at him. "What's God got to do with it? I imagine He's got bigger fish to fry than my screw ups."

"Don't be too sure about that? I believe God makes each one of us His first priority."

Les shook his head and tried to keep the smirk on his lips to a minimum. "I don't mean any disrespect, Judd, but that doesn't compute. This is a big world with billions of people."

"Yes, it is and the Creator of it is not Someone any of us can reason out in our human minds and make sense of Him. But anyone, anywhere in the world, who calls out to Him, He responds to that one as if no one else exists. That's how He makes us feel."

Both men were silent for a while.

"Les, have you ever met Jesus Christ?"

He shook his head uncomfortably and stared at the ground, thinking he needed to end this conversation. "Can't say that I have."

"Would you like to? He's got the help you need."

Les sat still and silent for a long time, then slowly stood up and made a decision at that moment to give Judd his resignation within a few days. Judd stood, too.

Les offered his hand and they shook firmly. "Thanks, Judd. I know you're trying to help, but I really need to go...too many loose ends today."

The preacher nodded and Les mounted up. He headed out at a lope without looking back.

Thankfully, Judd had to spend a minute or so to smother the fire before he left. He took his time, his heart heavy, feeling like he'd failed Les and God at the same time. He stayed on the ground beside his horse a while to keep from chasing after his foreman, to try harder to get him to listen. He looked up to see the young cowboy and Billy Joe disappear over the top of the ridge when he heard that unmistakable, still, small Voice, *My child was hungry and you fed him hope. Thank you.*

Eye's stinging, he blinked several times, swallowed hard and got on his horse. "Thank *You*, Lord."

Thankfully, none of the guys were at the barn when Les rode in to put his horse up. He would offer his apologies at the bunkhouse later.

Right now, determination was driving him to go home and get Kaitlyn's lunch and meds. The rest of the afternoon he intended to come up with a plan for where he would go from here. Once she was well enough to drive herself home, he would get her gone and then head out—somewhere.

For a long moment, Les stood in his kitchen door and stared inside. The mess he had left in there this morning was gone. Everything was clean as a whistle. And supper was simmering on the stove. It smelled like a delicious stew. A skillet of cornbread was sitting beside it. He stood there gritting his teeth so hard he thought they might break.

Obviously, Kaitlyn was feeling better. All this meant to him was getting this situation over with sooner than he expected. He didn't bother to wipe his boots at the door when he came in, never mind pull them off. His spurs jangled all the way down the hall announcing his boot tracked approach to the bedroom.

He came to a stop a couple of feet from the side of the bed. She appeared to be sound asleep where she lay on her side, on top of the quilt. She wore jeans rolled up to her calves and a soft yellow T-shirt. Her knees were drawn up, her feet bare, except for rosy colored toe nails. Her light brown curls were big and loose and feathered back away from her face.

Looking down at her, Les could easily entertain the idea of forgiving her for whatever fool stunt she had pulled with Jesse. But could he ever trust her? Did he really want to live his life with a woman who couldn't love him with any real depth to her feelings? She was a beautiful woman, but skin deep wasn't good enough. He rubbed a hand over his face, and then stared at her perfect little goddess form. He'd never seen anything so perfectly put together. How many years had he wasted broken up over this shallow little excuse? Too rich to become anything but spoiled. He had stood there long enough to work up a fresh batch of mad, when she opened her eyes.

"Les, you're home," she said without moving from her position on the bed. "Did you find your supper?"

"You're evidently feeling a lot better." He ignored her question.

"I was, but I guess I overdid it. I feel really tired."

"No big deal. If you need anything, I'll be on the couch." With that, he turned and walked out, spurs jingling the sound that Kaitlyn had loved to hear. But she felt like he'd just *jingled* in and slapped her.

She lay there barely breathing, staring at the empty space where he had just stood. The cold, blank look in his eyes was the worst possible reaction he could have shown toward her. She knew for certain that he knew about Jesse and he hated her.   A stony hardness settled over her, angry at the constant barrage of defeat that seemed to find its way into every good thing that tried to come into her life. Something had switched off inside of her.   A light went out, leaving a darkness so dense and heavy that she couldn't fight it. She felt a new kind of lonely. It was like a strengthening deep inside that stood up and fortified her, body and soul. She didn't understand what was happening inside of her at this moment, but she did know it was time to do what she had come here for in the first place.

Finally, something came easy. She sat up and let her head stop spinning, then headed to the den to face her last big giant.

Les was sitting on the couch holding a bottle of beer and staring sightlessly into the small flame in the fireplace.

Kaitlyn walked up in front of him and stared at his face until he looked up at her. Then she calmly and unemotionally spoke. "I came to Wyoming because I found out at the vet clinic in Joplin that you were here. I lived in a Christian rehab for depression for several months and had an assignment to accomplish after I came home. You were the last one on that assignment list. I came to find you to apologize. To ask your forgiveness for what I did to you. I blamed you for Mae-Belle and for her death hurting my dad. I was upset, but I was wrong in what I did to you. I went to your apartment the next day to apologize, but you were gone."

She paused a moment. He continued looking at her.

"I'm sorry I hurt you. I hope you'll forgive me." She had no tears. Her emotions were on hold, frozen. But she did mean what she said.

Without a word, Les moved to get up off the couch, causing her to take a step back. He went to the kitchen and set his half full beer bottle on the bar before pulling Kaitlyn's red journal out of the drawer he'd stuck it in. He returned to the den and handed it to her from an arm's length away. "You better take another look at that list you made in here and try again. Seems there's a point or two you haven't mentioned." He was glaring at her now.

She stood still, holding the book, never moving her eyes from his. "You...read my journal?" she asked softly, uncertain of how to approach the guts of her secrets with him. Baby Daniel and Jesse's names were on her list. And those two were the ones he had to be referring to. The others would be of no consequence.

She took a slow breath. She was very tired, in more ways than one, but she looked him straight in the eyes. "It was a silly mistake. I was with a couple of girlfriends. We came to Jesse's dude ranch to have some girl fun and I met Jesse. I was lonely and he was single. We went a little nuts, mistaking our need to have somebody special for...for love. It wasn't love... for either of us." She paused without blinking. His face hadn't softened any, but he was listening.

Surprised at how calm she felt, she continued. "We planned to be married after knowing each other only a few days. My friends went home and left me up here. Then one morning I realized the whole situation was wrong. So I got a ride to the Jackson airport and flew home. I never saw or heard from Jesse after that."

He continued to stare at her while he absorbed her story. Then after a long few seconds, "Did you have any intention of telling me about this when you came here?"

"No. As unbelievable as it might sound, I had forgotten about that event with Jesse altogether until I got to Jackson Hole and the familiar sights reminded me. I had only written his name on the list in this journal the morning of my accident....before I left the motel. I came here looking for you. To apologize to you."

"Did you and Jesse sleep together back then?" He knew the huge possibility of that, but wanted to get all the cards on the table.

"No, we didn't. Probably because I hadn't felt up to par the whole time I was at the ranch. I was sick for nearly a month after I got home."

She saw his face change for the first time. Surprise, maybe. Or relief. But it didn't matter at this point. Nothing felt like it would ever matter again.

"Katie, how could you have loved me enough to want to marry me, and then fall for another man so fast?"

The question gave her pause, but strangely didn't set off any ripples. "I didn't love Jesse. You had disappeared without a word and I was...on the rebound, I guess."

"I was here on this ranch working when you were with Jesse five miles up the road."

"I didn't know you were here, Les. I didn't know where you were. Odd coincidence."

"So, when do you plan on giving Jesse his apology?"

"I already did that."

Les stepped back like he was dodging a blow and waved his arm in the air. "Is that right," he smeared at her. "You came here to see me, and Jesse Brandon, the one you forgot about, got top billing." His face tightened. Then he suddenly remembered the cap. Jesse's cap laying in the kitchen floor that nobody seemed to know how it got there.

His eyes narrowed on her, an incredulous look that bored into her. "He was here, wasn't he? When you did your little, *I'm sorry,* for him. He was here, wasn't he?"

With eyes large and round at his outburst of rage, she nodded her head. "Yes. He was here."

Les didn't trust himself to say another word. Jesse had lied to him. Jesse. That made this entire mess a whole lot uglier. He had every intention of letting that holier-than-thou family man know what he thought of him.

Kaitlyn didn't want to leave anything else to have to be dealt with later. She had to tell him about their baby son. "Les…there's something else I…"

"No! I've heard enough. Go to bed and get some rest. It's about time you went home."

"But, I…"

"It's over, Katie."

"But…"

"I said drop it," he barked with teeth gritted.

She jumped, then headed for the bedroom and slammed the door.

***

CHAPTER NINE

It was 2 am when Jesse and Laura Brandon propped up in bed with pillows stuffed behind them and watched their newborn son greedily latch on to mom for his first middle of the night lunch. Jesse was up to offer moral support and do his diaper change duty.

Even though he had been so in to her and the kids from the beginning of their lives together, Laura was amazed at each event such as this. She'd had no idea marriage and family life could be this kind and sweet. Jesse was her one in a lifetime and she made sure he knew how deeply he was loved and respected.

She and Andy had walked right into a ready-made Heaven on earth, complete with a granny and later a gramps in Martha and Hank Walton.

And she had discovered there was a real God. He had to have planned all of this. It was too perfect. Too complete.

She looked up from watching her tiny infant suckling to find Jesse glowing into her face.

"If you could see your face right now. You've never looked so beautiful." He smiled lazily at her.

"I was just thinking about all of the blessings God has showered on us." She glanced back at the baby. "He is just the most recent one. There's been so many."

"Yes, there has and I thank Him daily for you and these kids and Hank and Martha and my little brother, Donny, whom I had better be hearing from before long, by the way. For two people who came together with no family, He just unloaded the truck at our door." Jesse wrinkled his nose in the air. "And speaking of unloading." They both laughed while Laura handed over the little *stinker.*

"Blessings to you, Dad," she giggled.

"Thanks…I think."

Laura got up, made a trip to the bathroom and looked in on Andy and Anna Leigh.

Hank and Martha had stayed over while she went to the hospital, but Jesse sent them home early this evening. Martha had seemed more tired than usual. Somewhat distracted.

Before she could get back to the bedroom, the office phone rang. Because it was nearly 3 am, she shuffled into the office and answered it.

She returned to the bedroom. Jesse had just put the sleeping baby in his bassinet and looked up at Laura's stricken expression.

"Honey?" He rushed to her, thinking she was sick or about to pass out and grasped her upper arms to steady her.

"That was Hank on the phone. He can't find Martha."

"What!?"

"He said she must have walked outside and walked away. Oh, Jesse."

He got Laura to the bed and grabbed his jeans and heavy long sleeved pullover shirt lying on the chair beside the bed. "Why would she do that?" He dressed in seconds. "How long has she been gone? My lord, it's three in the morning."

"I didn't question him. He sounded frantic. Not like Hank at all. I told him help was on the way."

Jesse kissed her quickly. "Will you be okay alone? Want me to call…"

"No. Go on. I'm good and Andy's here if I get in a bind. Go."

Jesse Jr. had made his debut into the world only a few hours ago, but the birth had been easy and Laura's strength returned almost immediatelynother place to be thankful to God. Andy's birth had been the complete opposite. She knew the difference and refused to be coddled and pampered when someone else was honestly in need of that attention. She fell asleep after praying for Martha.

Jesse slid his truck to a stop in front of Hank's cabin. Every light was on inside and out. He didn't bother to shut his truck door as he rushed inside.

"Hank!"

There was no answer and a ten second run through proved no one was here. Outside, Jesse stood still and could hear Hank calling for Martha. He ran, flashlight in hand, toward the sound and quickly caught up with him.

"Hank, what in blazes is going on?"

The elder cowboy's eyes were large and filled with fear. Jesse put a hand on his stooped shoulder in comfort.

"I can't find her, Jesse. She gets a little confused at times, but I'm scared about her now. At supper tonight, she didn't seem to know where she was. We went on to bed like usual and I woke up a little bit ago and she was gone. The front door was open. I turned ever light I have on, so maybe she'll see the light and come to it."

"How long has it been since you discovered she was gone?"

"Well, let's see. Long about an hour...Close to two now, maybe."

"Come back to the cabin with me and we'll call for some extra help." Jesse wasn't about to have both of them lost. When Hank hesitated, he said, "We'll find her much faster with all the boys out looking. Come on now. We're wasting precious time."

Hank reluctantly turned and followed. Jesse called Judd Luke, knowing he'd have a posse out within minutes. He turned to Hank and spoke in a quiet, calm voice, hoping to keep him from acting on the desperation showing in his tired, red-rimmed eyes. Jesse didn't remember him looking as old as he did tonight.

"Don't worry, Gramps. Granny Martha's a tough little lady. She'll be all right." Using their adopted names brightened his face a little. "You said she's been a little forgetful. How long has this been happening?"

"Not long, Jesse. But she wants to cry about things lately. I never knowed her to cry. But things set her off for no reason." Tears welled in Hank's eyes then and he turned his back to Jesse.

Jesse stood quietly and waited.

"She didn't know me today, Jesse. Her eyes were blank when she looked at me and she got scared and went to crying." Hank's voice was broken with emotion and Jesse fought to hold himself together. "I thought it would all pass. That she'd be all right in a little bit. So I put her to bed...and...now..."

Jesse was filled with controlled emotions as he listened to Hank's words. He felt his heart lurch in his chest, afraid this situation wasn't going to end well.

He heard the heavy vehicles coming up the road and sucked up his wilting heart, replacing it with a fresh *take-charge* demeanor. "Hank, I need you to stay here while me and these other men search the area. In case she comes back, somebody needs to be here. Got that?"

Reluctantly, he nodded his head, but Jesse wasn't convinced. He touched Hank's shoulder, turned him toward him and looked him in the eye. "Promise me you won't leave this house."

"I'll be here, Jesse. Oh, and that dog, Bonnie, might be with her. I tried calling her, but she don't usually come to me anyhow."

"That's good to know. If she shows back up here, honk one of the truck horns, long and loud."

He nodded again and Jesse wheeled around to meet the posse outside.

Two pickups and eleven cowboys filled up the front yard, including Judd Luke and Les Kane. Flashlights lit up the grounds as Jesse quickly explained the situation. Hank stood on the front porch and most of them shook his hand or patted his arm as they separated and headed out on foot. All ears were tuned to listen for any sound, including a dog barking.

Martha's name was called, breaking the silence across the darkness, again and again from all directions. Bonnie was called and whistled for. No one paired up, but scattered twelve different ways, woods and boulders, dips and hills apart.

After more than an hour of diligent searching, Rowdy Creed, the Double OO's newest and youngest wrangler, landed his beam of light in the eyes of a snarling, wild-eyed mongrel. It could have been mistaken for a wild dog the way every tooth in its head was threatening him and the hair was standing at attention on the back of its neck. The dog growled with more ferocity than Rowdy thought a domestic animal could have. But he knew beyond a doubt this was Bonnie. She fit the description they were given, right down to the pink collar around her neck.

Rowdy squatted down and called softly to her, but she only growled more viciously. She seemed to be protecting something. He moved slowly, giving the dog a wide berth where he could shine his flashlight behind her into a crevice of large rocks. A wildlife path curved through the rocks. Rowdy moved the light beam up the path until it shone on bloody bare feet sticking out beneath a dirty white gown.

"Oh, my Lord," Rowdy felt his heart skip against his chest. He took a step forward, forgetting the dog until the dog reminded him. He called out, "Ms. Martha? Ms. Martha? Can you hear me?"

There was no answer or movement.

Bonnie turned and trotted over to where Martha lay and stood her ground, teeth bared.

The young cowboy backed away in an attempt to settle the dog, then walked several yards to a hilly clearing. Cupping his mouth with both hands, he yelled several times, turning different directions. "Over here. I found her. Over here."

"Keep talking," shouted a voice way out in the darkness.

"Here. Over here. Over here."

Finally, several lights cut through the blackness. Judd was first to reach his wide-eyed, excited cowhand. "Where is she?" Judd waved his light out in the dark. Several more lights joined his, including Jesse's.

"Mr. Luke, the dog is with her and she wouldn't let me get to Ms. Martha. The lady is laying on the ground over here."

Rowdy headed off at a fast clip to where he first encountered the dog, the rest of the crew following.

Out of the dark brush shot Bonnie, teeth bared and snarling like she meant business. Cowboy's scattered. A few curses were let loose.

"Everybody stay back a ways." Jesse moved toward Rowdy. "Go easy and show me where you saw her, son."

Taking the wide way around, Rowdy shined a light on Martha's feet. Immediately, Bonnie took up her guard position, crouching and snarling almost on top of Martha's unmoving legs.

"Martha, it's Jesse. Can you hear me?"

No response.

"I'm going to my truck for a rifle." Jesse started to go when Les Kane stepped forward.

"Wait, Jesse. That dog is protecting her the only way she knows how. Hank might be able to call her off."

"No. That old man will rush in there, dog attack or not. I know him."

"Then let me get Kaitlyn out here. That was her dog and she led us to where Katie had fallen off of the ledge. She might come to her."

"All right, go get her and hurry. I'll get my gun just in case that doesn't work and call for an ambulance."

Les blew through his front door like he had a hurricane-sized tailwind on his butt. He didn't realize at first that Kaitlyn was fully dressed and standing in the kitchen. He stopped, startled, then grabbed her arm and hauled her toward the front door. He grabbed up a quilt lying on the couch as he passed by it.

"Les! Have you lost your mind?" She stumbled, almost falling.

"Just come on, I'll explain on the way. This is an emergency."

"Can I at least get my coat?"

"I have an extra one in the truck." He half dragged her, never slowing down.

In less than ten minutes, Les and Kaitlyn were running through brush and rocks and woods to where the others were waiting. Understanding the serious time situation, Kaitlyn went straight to the spot Les pointed to and called to Bonnie. There didn't seem to be one good breath sucked in by the entire group of men as they waited and listened for the dog.

"Bonnie? Come here, baby. It's okay now. Come on," she cooed to her until a faint whining was heard in the rocks. The whimpering came from Bonnie. Kaitlyn girded herself for what she might see and walked straight toward the sound without hesitation. Les followed behind with a flashlight so she could see where to walk, the quilt rolled up under his arm.

Judd turned to the solemn assembly of young cowboys who had just joined him in a prayer for Martha and pointed to two of them. "A.J....Rowdy, you two head back to Hank's place. One of you stay with him and keep him there. The other one bring the EMT's out here."

Both took off at a fast pace.

In the near distance, emergency sirens were blaring, red and blue lights twinkling through the trees from the highway.

Jesse followed Les and Kaitlyn, carrying a blanket he had pulled out of the back seat of his truck. He left his rifle with Judd.

Martha was shivering and trying to speak. All three had slipped out of their coats. The two men worked, getting her wrapped up in the quilts and coats.

"Hang in there, Granny Martha," Jesse spoke close to her ear. "We've got you now. You're going to take a little ambulance ride, but you'll be all right." Jesse pulled his heavy shirt over his head and wadded it for a makeshift pillow for her head, then stood up to let Les have room to check her vitals.

Les had noticed that her body was fairly warm for the 35 degrees of the early morning. Her pulse was strong as well. They opted to not move her in case she'd fallen against one of the boulders she was laying between and broke a bone. The paramedics would be better to check her for injury.

He stood up from his quick assessment to find that Jesse, wearing only a short sleeved T-shirt, had moved over beside Kaitlyn where she held Bonnie in her arms. Jesse's arm was wrapped snugly around Katie, his hand rubbing up and down her bare arm.

Kaitlyn saw the fury in Les's gaze, but she didn't move. *That* seemed so not important at the moment.

"Will she be all right, Les?" She asked in all sincerity for the sweet little lady whom Bonnie had claimed for her very own person.

"Physically she seems to be strong." Les fought in himself to keep the beloved little woman lying at his feet in perspective to the angry riot in his head at the audacity of Jesse Brandon's move on Katie. Oh, he realized she only wore a short sleeved thin sweater and it was cold out here, but Jesse's arms had held her before in a different context. The idea made him livid.

Les's glance of anger wasn't lost on Jesse. He saw it and felt Kaitlyn tense against his side. Did she tell him, he wondered, about their fifteen minutes of idiocy years back? Even so, that couldn't be the problem. Lover's spat, he decided and forgot it.

Kaitlyn took herself and Bonnie out of the way of the emergency crew and law enforcement that were crowded around. As soon as she stepped back into the clearing, where the ranch hands were all still waiting, jackets began unzipping. The closest man to her was Judd and he settled his warm down jacket around her and helped her maneuver the dog from one arm to the other to get the jacket on.

"Thank you, Mr. Luke."

"You're welcome, Kaitlyn." He ruffled Bonnie on the head. "This little gal scared a month of Sunday's out of these big tough cowboys here. Ms. Martha will be proud when she finds out how well she was guarded."

Katie gave the dog a hug. "I think she was meant to be here for Ms. Martha all along…maybe to help save her life tonight. Les said Martha was warmer than she should have been. And her white gown is matted with Bonnie's fur where she must have lain on top of her."

Judd's eyes widened at that. "Wow. I've heard of animals taking care of their people like that. But I've never actually witnessed it before."

Kaitlyn had believed that God sent her to Wyoming to complete a healing process in her. It hadn't occurred to her that this little dog running out in the road in front of her car may have actually been foreseen and used by the Lord to bring Kaitlyn the whereabouts of Les *and* get the little accident victim to Wyoming for Ms. Martha. The whole thing was too exact, including the timing, to have been a coincidence.

Les appeared at that moment, just ahead of the stretcher bearing Martha. She was fully conscious and not liking all the fuss being made over her.

Bonnie heard the familiar voice and almost jumped out of Kaitlyn's arms to get to her owner.

"Hold up a sec." Jesse stopped the procession carrying the patient. "Bring that pup over here, Katie."

Kaitlyn held the excited little caregiver and let her and Martha reunite. Bonnie licked Martha's face making her giggle like a little girl. It brought chuckles and grins throughout the whole group.

Word had been sent to Hank that his wife seemed to be all right. He was waiting with A.J. at the edge of the woods behind his cabin when the group emerged from the quarter mile trek. They stopped again long enough for Hank to grab is wife's face in his shaky hands and plant a long, slow kiss on her lips.

"Let her up for air, Cook, before I have to go hunt up some oxygen," one of the hands quipped.

Laughter and a few whoops sounded until Hank rose up and the breaking daylight flickered across his wet streaked cheeks. The silent *I love you* that glittered between the aging couple quieted the atmosphere, except for the ear splitting sound of breaking hearts and memories surfacing—some good, some bad. Every man and woman on earth desires what they'd just witnessed on this beloved, well-respected couple, including every rangy Wyoming cowboy, no matter their age or background.

Judd had tried to teach this kind of love at his cowboy church gatherings, but Hank and Martha had just done it in a way he could never get across in words.

Kaitlyn buried her face in Bonnie's fur, trying to stifle the sob that was filling her throat. She felt a strong comforting arm encircle her shoulders. Les had just told her it was time for her to go back to Missouri. She wasn't sure how she felt about his comforting move on her now.

She glanced up. It wasn't Les, but Jesse. He was swallowing fast and hard and she offered a hug by laying her head against his shoulder for a quick moment. A glance to the opposite side of her caught Les standing in the middle of his men, staring at her and Jesse. It wasn't anger she saw this time, but pain. The same hurt she'd seen years ago when her beautiful engagement ring hit him in the face.

Without a word to anyone, Les passed in front of her, patted Hank on the shoulder as he went by and walked toward his truck. By the time the rest got to the waiting ambulance and their vehicles, Les had left.

Judd followed the ambulance carrying Martha and Hank to the hospital while Kaitlyn helped Jesse close up their little cabin. Bonnie had been deposited in Jesse's truck for safe keeping.

Jesse had already realized that Les had left Katie to fend for herself. He didn't know the extent of their relationship, but he did know that Les had gone after her and brought her out here, and then drove off and left her.

"Hop in, Miss Grace." Jesse tried to keep the situation light hearted. "I know I'm not the one that brung ya, but I'm more than happy to take you back."

She couldn't keep from smiling. She remembered so well why she had fallen for this sweet, funny cowboy, so long ago. He had become her friend now and that felt so wonderful. There was nothing she needed more right now than a friend.

"How is Laura and the baby?"

"Doing great. Laura came home in a few hours after the birth, running around like nothing happened." He cut his eyes at her. "Well, almost."

She smiled and nodded.

"So, what's happening in your world, Katie?"

Burdening Jesse with her mess didn't feel right. She lightened it up as best she could. "Well, to paraphrase my itinerary, I was heading home to Missouri this morning. Car is all packed up. And, by the way, thank you so much for your help and friendship while I've been here, Jesse. I wish I'd been able to meet your family."

"So do I. You would like Laura." A frown creased his brow as he looked out at the highway where he was driving and back at her. "I guess I thought you and Les were becoming a couple. I was sort of hoping that for the both of you."

She didn't want to go into detail or talk about Les right now. Her emotions were parked on *dull* and she preferred to keep them there. It was easier to cope with having to leave this beautiful country—and Les. What was there to say? He had his life to get on with and she had hers, whatever it turned out to be. She didn't get an opportunity to tell Les that she had given birth to his son. She still believed he had a right to know about Danny, but she didn't know how to get there from here. Not now.

"That's not meant to be for me and Les." It hurt to say it.

"Well, I won't pry anymore. But I do have to ask you one more question."

"What's that?"

"Are you planning to take Bonnie back to Missouri with you?"

"Oh!" She twisted around to look at the sleeping little fur ball in the back seat. "I...I don't know. Oh, Jesse, I can't separate her and Martha."

"No, that would devastate both of them. Tell you what. I'll take her on home with me and see to her until Martha and Hank can take her back."

"Do you think Martha will be all right?"

"We'll have to wait and see what the doctors come up with. Hopefully it's an easy fix."

"I'll put her in my prayer journal."

He nodded and smiled wistfully. "I'll tell her that for you."

When they arrived at Les's cabin, the sun was rising and his truck was gone. Or never came home.

Kaitlyn said her good-byes to Jesse and Bonnie and went inside for a quick run through in case she'd missed packing something. She hesitated, thinking she should at least leave a thank you note for Les, but decided against it. She got in her car, knowing she had left him something much bigger than a note. She'd left her heart in there.

***

CHAPTER TEN

There's no place like home. That's what they say, anyway, Kaitlyn thought. But they, whoever *they* are, couldn't prove it by me. She closed her eyes and let a ragged sigh escape.

It had taken the month that she had been home in Joplin to get settled in. But she wasn't home. She'd never felt like she belonged here. There were no good memories to draw from that bonded her to either her mom or dad. The saddest thing in the world was having this overwhelming desire to go home, but having no clue where home was.

She had numbly kept herself busy during the past days and fell exhausted into bed at night—anything to keep her mind off of Les. She cleaned the ranch house from top to bottom, restocked the kitchen and tonight she sat curled up in front of the blazing gas log fireplace feeling more alone than she ever had in her life.

She had driven to Wyoming and fulfilled her last assignment. The one that was supposed to free her soul so she could get on with her life. Start anew. And yet, she was worse off now than before. But she knew why.

Les Kane. The pain in his eyes the last time she saw him haunted her. She should have gone after him. Or waited until he came home and tried to explain things better. To tell him she loved him more than life. To make him understand that she'd made a foolish and childish decision when she'd planned to marry Jesse, an event she barely remembered.

She had picked up the phone to call Les several times, but always stopped herself before punching in all the numbers. He had told her to leave his home. She did leave and he hadn't tried to call her. Nothing made any sense. She seemed to be doomed to a life of loneliness and rejection, but something inside her was refusing to accept that verdict.

She picked up her red journal and flipped its pages. On the inside of the back cover she wrote in large letters the strange words she'd heard spoken inside of her while sitting in Les's kitchen. *Bone of my bones, flesh of my flesh.* Then she laid the book back onto the lamp table beside her chair.

Please, Lord, tell me what I'm supposed to do now. I have no one but You. Are you here, Lord? Are You even here?

She leaned her head onto the side of her big recliner and cried.

Be still and know that I Am God.

Les squeezed his eyes shut as tight as he could. But when he opened them, she was still there, laying on the rocky ledge below him, soaking wet and not moving.

He stared into the darkness from his bed, that image of Kaitlyn when he had first laid eyes on her again, would not go away. He was not dreaming. He was wide awake, the image embedded in his mind in the dark space out in front of him. He didn't know how he was viewing this scene, but it was relentless in harassing him. Day or night, he got no break except when sheer exhaustion claimed him.

For weeks, ever since the night he'd come home from stringing and restringing fence until his gloves ripped and his fingers bled, the end of the same day that Martha Walton had gotten lost, he'd wallowed in a bitter anger. He worked from before daylight to way after dusk. As long as he kept moving and kept his distance from socializing, he could manage the heartache. But this vision of her helpless body alone and needing somebody to rescue her was quickly bringing him to the end of himself. He just didn't know what to expect when his end came.

He got up and dragged his worn out self into the kitchen. Days old food he'd left out on the stove and the bar stunk. Crud of some kind was sticking to the bottom of his bare feet from the floor. When he looked up at the wall clock over the window, he couldn't see the time. He saw Katie's body laying helpless on the ledge.

He grabbed his head with both hands and let out a guttural moan of despair. A string of curses bounced off the walls around him.

Within ten minutes he was dressed, in his truck and heading through the rough, bone-jarring pasture to the valley on the back ninety. He parked his truck on the ridge just above the valley, got out and traipsed through the trees a short piece until he reached the tent.

Judd had set up this one room canvas tent as his *escape* several years ago. It was his sanity getaway, he'd called it, to hide from the world when it got too rough to live in. Les had used it before, but it had been a while.

It was cold, but he couldn't feel it. He grabbed up the dusty blankets that stood in for a bed, took them outside and shook the dust into the southbound breeze. There was just enough moonlight to half see what he was doing. A kerosene Coleman lantern hung inside but he didn't want a light. A Coleman burner set on a table inside as well, but cold and dark seemed befitting for how he felt. In fact, he'd never been in so dark a place inside himself before.

He lay on the blankets he'd haphazardly tossed back inside feeling like he'd received a good solid punch in his gut. He'd found the only woman he would ever love. And he'd lost her. Not once, but twice.

Even though he was dressed to be out in the cold, his insulated long handles under jeans and a heavy cotton denim shirt, all tight around him under a weatherproof down jacket, didn't hold any warmth around his heart. The depth of that chill should have lessened after suffering years already. But it didn't. A little *faux* hope for a few days and he was in worse shape than before. *Is this the kind of God You are?* He ranted inwardly at nothing because there was nothing to hear him.

Son, you rejected My help.

As soon as those words rose up inside of his being, he saw an image in his mind of him and Judd sitting beside the branding pit talking. His eyes popped wide open. After a few seconds, he sat straight up on his pallet and began to shiver, feeling the cold for the first time. Did he just imagine those words? Son? Not once in his life could he remember ever being afraid in the dark until this moment.

He got up and walked out into the light of the moon. His heart was pounding a hole in his chest. What was happening to him? Desperation swamped him. He set out at a fast stride through the trees to his truck. His hands shook so hard he could hardly get his key into the ignition.

Finally, he tore out of there with his headlights on bright and didn't slow down until he pulled up in front of the Luke's big log home. He didn't consider the time of night. It never crossed his mind. He *had* to see Judd, *now*.

He hit the truck lights and switch, jumped out and bolted to the front door. He pushed the doorbell over and over, even though he could clearly hear it ring each time. The porch light was on and a floodlight bathed the yard. He hit the bell again almost at the same instant that lights came on inside the house.

Judd opened the front door, already having seen Les from

the window. "Les?" Judd pushed open the outer storm door and took a step to the side. "Come in here out of the cold."

Les went inside and stood, having no idea what to say. But just standing there with his boss seemed to give him a renewed sense of sanity. He took off his hat and nervously rolled it in his hands by the brim. "I'm sorry about this, Judd. I don't even know what time it is."

Judd knew. He'd seen that same stark fear on men before. Les was on a round up tonight, only he was the one being chased and corralled. "Come in and sit down."

Les couldn't sit. In fact, he was feeling ridiculous and too hot now that he'd barged in on this family at God knows what hour of the night.

Judd sensed Les was about to bolt. He grabbed his heavy coat off the rack by the door and slid it on over his T-shirt and sweat-pants. His socks would have to do for his feet. "Come on," he said and led the way out the front door to the front porch swing. "Have a seat."

They sat in silence for a couple of minutes, Les not knowing what to say and Judd praying for God to give him right words to say.

Finally, Judd turned to look straight at Les. "Tell me what happened to you tonight."

Les swallowed hard at the lump that was blocking his composure. "The other day when we talked, you asked me if I wanted to…well, to meet God. You know…Jesus?"

Judd nodded to urge him on.

"Well, I didn't. I didn't see much need for all that." He swallowed. "I mean, I believe in God. I know He's up there running this world. But…tonight I went up to your tent on the back ninety. I couldn't sleep. Too much on my mind and I…well, I was laying there and I kinda let God have it. I was just thinking how He wasn't much of a God. Then I…well, I *think* I heard Him talk to me. He just came right into the tent with me."

It was all Judd could do to keep a straight face. This sounded just like the God he knew. He will certainly come and meet you where you're at! "What did He say, Les?"

"He called me *son* and said I had rejected His help. I got scared, Judd. I was scared laying there in the dark. I've never been afraid of the dark in my life. I've always thought that people who hear voices like that are mentally unstable. You know… nuts!"

Judd couldn't keep from chuckling. "Well, I've got good news to tell you. I hear God speak to me sometimes and I haven't gone around the loony bend yet. Actually, the Bible plainly says, *My sheep hear My Voice.* That's in the book of John in Chapter 10. Jesus is called the Good Shepherd and we are His sheep. But if He said you rejected His help, then I can help you correct that right now. Have you ever asked Jesus to forgive your sins and help you live the way He wants you to live?"

Les shook his head. "No, I've never done that."

For the next few minutes, Judd explained why Jesus came to earth and why He died on the cross and rose again to life eternal. "He's offering you that eternal life with Him in Heaven just by simply saying *yes* to His offer."

Les felt like he couldn't wait a second longer. Something inside of him was calling him, pulling him, compelling him until refusing to respond would have taken a stronger will than he had. He suddenly was desperate to know this Person who talked to him in that tent in the woods. "I want that, Judd. I want to know Jesus. I *have* to know Him."

Judd's insides were turning somersaults. He fought to hold his emotions intact. To watch the Holy Spirit of God fall so heavily on a man, especially one of these tough, hard-driving cowboys was humbling. His heart swelled with thankfulness to God for allowing him the honor of bringing another one of His children Home. "Let's bow our heads and tell Him that. I'll help you pray if you want me to."

Les couldn't speak, but nodded his head. He slipped off of the swing onto his knees, nearly causing Judd to let go of the tears that had been threatening him.

Judd joined him there and even before that prayer was ended, both cowboys were openly weeping before God as one repented and the other was just overjoyed.

They talked for a while before Les drove back to his cabin and slept, exhausted, but peaceful, the rest of the night.

Kaitlyn could hear the accusing voices of everyone she'd ever loved. All dead now or gone away. But they were all around her, gathered together, fingers pointing toward her face. She slapped at the distorted figures that hovered over her, and then she screamed, "Jesus." The sound of her own voice brought her bolt upright. Her face was tear-streaked, her breath shallow. The fire was still flickering over the fake logs, but she felt so cold, so rejected and forsaken. It was just a nightmare. Or was it?

How could she have spent so much time believing He was leading her steps, guiding her up out of a lifelong hopeless pit, filling her insides with so much joy and hope, then grab her up and slam her back to the reality of—what? That she wasn't worthy? She'd simply made too many mistakes. Even God couldn't completely redeem her.

Every muscle in her body was screaming at her when she stood up from the ages old recliner where her dad had spent a lot of his last months. She had to get a grip. She felt old and worn out.

Even though her heart felt like a dead weight, she forced her body, through sheer willpower, to bend and move under her direction toward the kitchen for a strong cup of coffee. She would start there and then make some decisions for herself.

She sat at the breakfast table in her spotless ranch style kitchen. The early morning sun was showing under the partially opened mini blinds, but she had no desire to let in the light.

Her eyes traveled around the perimeter of the room trying to find something that would trigger a happy, homey memory. Something to build on to get her day motivated.

Where are you looking, My child?

A slow dawning began to quietly ease into her mind. A thought. Her slumped shoulders rose as she pulled her bent frame up straight. Then she saw clearly. She was looking for her moment, her day, for her future, in her past. She had taken a step backward without realizing it. All of her past fears and tormenting times had come in her dreams to warn her not to come back there.

She got it. This part of her life was finished. This house. The ranch. All of it was in her past. Internally, she had already left this place. There was nothing here for her anymore.

With a fresh surge of hopeful energy, she jumped up and grabbed a phone book off of the desk behind her. Two hours later, she led Mackenzie Layne, an eager young cowgirl-type realtor around the entire property, inside the house, barn and acreage. Only the quarter acre on the north corner of the ranch, the family cemetery, was not included. No matter where she went from here, she respectfully vowed to see that that small area was well kept as a memorial to her family.

She hadn't felt so right about a thing since she got home from Wyoming.

There wasn't an inkling in her of where she would go after the ranch sold. But at the moment, it didn't matter that much. Without Les, anywhere would serve as somewhere. Except for the Grace home place. Walking away from here would be easy. Learning to live her daily existence without Les Kane would be the hard place. But she had managed it before. She could do it again.

"It's been a pleasure, Miss Grace." Mackenzie shook hands with her new client. "I'll get this contract ready for your signature and my sign posted out front today." She was thoughtful for a moment. "Now, you did say that you could be ready to vacate this property on as short a notice as we needed? Is that right?"

Kaitlyn nodded. "Yes. Seeing as I'm only packing a few pictures and clothes. Everything else stays with the house."

"Well, then I'll tell you now that I do have a client who is looking for a small ranch about this size. So, as soon as you and I are squared away with the paperwork, I'll give them a call. Your place could show as soon as tomorrow or the next day."

"Works for me. Thank you and I'll be by your office this afternoon."

For the rest of the morning, Kaitlyn went through the house and took pictures off the walls and furniture tops. All of her dad's, as well as Wade's personal effects had already been stored or done away with. Her mom had her own bedroom for a while, even before Wade's death. Her things were all just as she'd left them.

She stood in the center of Rebecca's immaculately kept space and fought with herself over what she should do. Finally, she decided to pack away everything, except the furniture, and rent a storage locker for it in case her mom came back. She knew her mom was sick. Her life's experiences had taken a toll on her mind, leaving her unforgiving and bitter.

Kaitlyn knew she had initially been headed down that same road. But God! Why He chose to rescue her and not her mother, she often wondered. But she'd learned in rehab that God will make an offer to help us, but then we have to choose to allow His help or not. God is a Gentleman. He doesn't force His Will over our own. But, He does require that we accept His help, His way...not ours. Sometimes that can be hard to accept.

At any rate, her mom's personal stuff would be kept for her, just in case.

Everything in her dad's desk and file cabinets had been dealt with over time. She was grateful for that.

That afternoon, she drove into Joplin and stopped by Ms. Layne's office, signed her contract after an hour of reading and discussing her options. Then she stuffed some packing boxes into her car and went home to begin the finish of her physical life in the only home she had ever known.

After three days of packing and rummaging through the house and barn, she was satisfied that she was ready to hand over the house key.

A contract had been placed on the ranch the day after she'd called the realtor. Surveyors had come and gone. She was just biding her time, having no direction to go anyway. She thought it strange that she had no concern that any day she would be homeless with nothing but herself behind the wheel of her car. That would be the day that the strength of her trust in God would be sorely tested. Was He that personal of a God that He would lead her to someplace? Would she find out He didn't really care where she went to live?

Ever since Les had landed on the Double OO ranch in Wyoming, he'd hardly been farther than twenty miles from it and that had been on veterinary business. He'd lived like a recluse and liked every month and year of it.

The ranch work slowed down a little in winter, giving him extra time on his hands. It was nearly Christmas and this was the first year he could recall caring, especially since he was grown and alone.

Judd had dropped off a small stack of books and leaflets at the cabin the day after Les had given himself to Jesus. One was a Bible and one was a story book about Christmas and the birth of Jesus. It was a child's book that Judd said his daughter, Abby, had sent. Inside the cover was a child's printed inscription: To Mr. Les, From Abby Luke. He read the Christmas story three times, amazed at what was happening inside of him. The more he read about Jesus, the more he *wanted* to read and to understand. He read the pamphlets about God's love for mankind. One taught about forgiving those who had wronged you and one talked about prayer. He read those until he could almost recite them by memory. The Bible, he read off and on. It was harder to get, yet he couldn't seem to leave it alone.

But today, he wasn't in the mood to read. He was bundled up in his big winter coat and hat, walking, more like pacing, down to the pond and back, around the house, through his back door and out the front again.

Somewhere deep inside himself, he was being strongly compelled to *go see Jesse*. He didn't want to go see Jesse. He let that business go a few weeks ago. But it was about to drive him nuts, so after the second trip around the house and back out the front door, he got in his truck and pointed it that way.

He knew he had to face what had happened, even though he didn't know what had happened. He figured he was about to get in on the details.

Before he got to High Point, it popped into his mind to pray. He wasn't sure he knew how to pray about this. Then he repeated these words that had just whispered through his thoughts: *Lord Jesus, take control of mine and Jesse's conversation. Amen.*

Not sure he prayed the right way, he pushed that out of his head and within a minute, pulled up in front of Jesse's barn. It surprised him when Jesse stepped through the doorway and motioned him inside, smiling.

Les got out and followed him over to where a few bales of hay had been dragged into a circle for sitting. Jesse handed him a smoking mug of coffee and they both sat opposite each other.

Les looked a little dumbfounded. "Were you expecting somebody?"

"You." Jesse replied and blew steam over the rim of his coffee cup.

This was too strange for Les to let it go. "How…did you know I was coming?"

"Truthfully? God told me."

Les went blank. Was he being made fun of? "I don't get it."

"Well, tell me something. What made you drive over here?"

Les thought a minute, his eyes rounding at the realization. "I just…felt something. I don't know."

Jesse smiled. "The Lord's not always that obvious, Les. Most times I think we just sort of move through our day and He accomplishes His Will in us when we don't even know He's doing it. But other times, like today, He speaks inside us or strongly compels us to do a certain thing."

"Is that why I was a sack of jumping beans just before I headed over here?"

Jesse laughed loudly. "I reckon so. It got you here."

Les looked at him stupidly. "Did you get the jumping beans to know I was on my way?"

Jesse laughed again. This newly converted cowboy was a hoot. "Not exactly. It was kind of strange though. He just downloaded the information into me all at once. Maybe He said the words. It's hard to explain what He does. But all of a sudden, I knew you were coming over here to see me, so being the gracious host that I am, I had us some coffee hot and poured up."

Les, feeling a little freaked, took a big gulp of coffee then and fried his tongue.   Jesse lost it that time and nearly rolled off his hay bale. Then his cup of hot coffee sloshed on his jeans immediately scalding his inner thigh. He yelped and jumped to his feet, slapping his leg and hopping around like he had gone up in flames.

Both men laughed long and loud and got rid of the boiling liquid before they killed themselves.

With the ice, plus a little skin, thoroughly melted between the two, Jesse spoke up. "We both know why we need to talk, Les."

Les nodded and stared at the ground trying to collect his thoughts. He wasn't sure he wanted to have this conversation. "None of that matters now. She's gone and that's done with."

"Evidently, the Lord knows something you don't because He set this meeting up. Let's just let Him finish what He started here. First and foremost, I want you to know that Kaitlyn and I never slept together. We shared a few kisses. But that's as far as it went. That little fling lasted two weeks, the last week or so of it, she was sick nearly every day. She had a stomach bug or something. I thought she was a knockout and she thought I was a handsome devil, so we acted like two school kids on spring break."

Les kept his eyes on the floor. "Did you love her, Jesse?"

"I thought so at the time. But when Laura showed up I realized I'd never experienced being in love before. Kaitlyn didn't love me either. She didn't even tell me her real name. I knew her as Katie Lynn. That's how serious she wasn't. She had a crush, but I knew the whole time that something or someone else was on her mind. I tried to ignore it, but when she left suddenly, I knew it was for the best."

"I heard you were heartbroken for a long time after she left."

"Yeah, well, wasn't my heart after all. My pride took a butt kicking. Laura's the only woman to ever have my heart. And that's because she was chosen by the Lord to be my wife and me to be her husband. It has to do with a Bible verse that says something about *Bone of my bones and flesh of my flesh.*"

Les had no idea what he meant by *bones* and *flesh* and didn't question it. His face creased in hard angry lines. "Why did you lie about being in my house the day I found your cap in my kitchen floor?"

Surprise widened Jesse's eyes. "I didn't lie."

Les's face grew livid. "She told me, Jesse. Katie told me you were there at the house when she made an apology to you for running out on you. With you lying about it, a man has to wonder what else happened there that day." Les knew she had been sick as a hound dog that same day, but he didn't say so.

Jesse looked up into the space of the barn as he tried to recall the events. Then he looked back at his accuser. "I *was* at your place the day she did that. She was down by the pond and I rode up on Boss, headed for Judd's barn. We talked a minute and she did offer an apology to me. I accepted it and that was that. Except, my little son came *driving* up to tell me Laura had taken a fall at the house. I remember chunking Boss's reins to Katie and hauling for home with Andy. You know the rest."

He looked surprised and unnerved. That's what she meant when she said he'd been there. "All right, I get that. But…how did your cap get to my house?"

Jesse hesitated several seconds. "Les, I'm not one to pass along gossip. So I'm hoping that's not what I'm about to do.

But I do believe you're owed an explanation. The day my cap disappeared from under my nose inside this barn, I had a visitor puttering around in here. And the day I drove Kaitlyn to Jackson Hole to pick up her car, that same visitor was in the Burger Gittin Place when I took her in for a bite to eat." He paused and kicked some loose hay around with his boot. "Short of it is, he was a little rude for my taste."

"Rude to Kaitlyn?"

Jesse nodded.

"Cory Raye. It was Cory, wasn't it?"

"Yes, but I had a little *come to Jesus* meeting with him a couple days later and I tricked him into confessing to taking my hat and chunking it inside your back door. I suspected him from the start. I told him Kaitlyn was there at the time, making him believe she saw him. He was just trying to stir the pot. Make some trouble for…"

"Wait. Hold on a minute. Stir what pot?"

"Cory took Kaitlyn to the airport that day. He's been known around here to make mischief from time to time."

Les frowned trying to get the point. "But, why would he attack her over giving her a lift to the airport?"

"He had some notion in his head that my honor needed defending. But, fact is, there are people in the world who seem to thrive on creating destruction in other's lives. That boy *way* overstepped his boundary this time. Judd and I showed him to the gate a few weeks ago. We both agreed to keep on praying for him and told him so. Some people have to learn their lessons the hard way."

Les was quiet for a long time. "This Christian life is hard to do. It would be easier to just punch his lights out and be done."

Jesse howled. "Man, you got that right. Way easier."

Les stood, offered his hand to Jesse and without another word, walked out and went home.

The evening found Les sitting outside with a large mug of hot coffee and his mind running amuck. Loneliness was painful and it had smooth run him down just as soon as he'd let his anger slide away. He knew this would happen if he stopped despising and blaming Kaitlyn for five minutes. Since returning home from his talk with Jesse, his stewing had idled down to a gentle calm.

Everything had ceased to exist, except his memories, particularly of the past couple of weeks of his life. He knew his life was nothing without Kaitlyn.

He kept remembering the way she looked when he'd first seen her in the barn at the Grace ranch. The sexy little siren worked hard to put it on him. And did she ever! He remembered the way she looked when he'd found her on the ledge in the storm, fearing at first that she might be dead. He could feel, even now, how tightly she'd clung to him when he had found her scared to death in the dark woods behind his cabin. He could see her standing in his kitchen making cookies. Burning cookies. Twice! That memory split his face into a grin.

He rose from his chair on the back porch, went inside and showered. After donning his best jeans and a black pullover sweater, he pulled a suitcase from his closet and began stuffing extra clothes and bathroom stuff into it before he even paused to check out what he was doing.

He was going to get his woman. That's what he was doing. His arms and legs had started the process, seemingly of their own volition. Now that his brain had caught up, an energetic hope filled his whole being.

He raced through the house on a cleaning spree, wiping, mopping and fixing until he was satisfied that it was passable. He had every intention of bringing Katie back home with him. He didn't want to gross her out as soon as he got her here.

He stood back and looked. Satisfied that it would at least halfway pass muster, he grabbed his bag, closed up the cabin and headed out.

He stopped at Judd and Toni's to let them know he had to be gone a few days. When Toni swung the front door open, a strong aroma of cookies baking hit him in the nose. She had a doughy spatula in one hand and white flour across her nose. A red, flour-splattered apron with green and white Christmas trim covered her clothes.

He gave her a message for Judd, then giddy-like, grabbed her in a quick bear hug, said *thank you,* and left.

Toni's eyes were as huge as the grin on her face as she watched this new boy of God's hurry to his truck. She knew that *in love* kind of happy when she saw it. She blinked away the tears and whispered, "Bless him, Lord. Bless him."

Les raced into Jackson Hole to fulfill the idea Toni Luke had just given him. He would feel silly about the way he was behaving, except he was just too happy to care.

Thankfully, the Corner Supermarket was still open. He raced around inside and gathered up all the ingredients of Kaitlyn's favorite cookie recipe, plus a few more items for a couple days' worth of meals. A pot of poinsettias finished his spree.

He hauled back home and put everything up, but left the cookie making items sitting on the kitchen bar beside the Christmas flowers. Perfect! *Les, you are one romantic cuss!*

The sun was down by the time he headed for Missouri.

The ranch sold. Kaitlyn thought she should feel some kind of loss in this event, but she didn't. This season of her life was so done and over, even to her bone marrow.

She had up to thirty days to vacate the property. She decided to wait a few days and clean up the little cemetery to her liking. She had a heavy-duty white vinyl ranch style fence installed to border it and clean white rock to cover each grave. She washed the headstones and bought each spot its own individual color of fresh flowers. Those flowers were intermingled with artificial fall leaves and greenery, so when the live plants were wilted and gone, there would still be a mingling of color.

Special care was given to the last grave on the end of the row. A tiny grave that she was so slowly and lovingly placing an intermingling of pale blue stones throughout the white rock, when her cell phone rang. The ID showed it was her Realtor.

"Hi, Mackenzie."

"Hi. I'm here at the house and a man is here waiting for you. Are you...?"

"Oh, that's the man who put in the fence. Tell him I'm out at the cemetery. Thanks, Ms. Layne."

She stuck her phone back in her pocket and got back on her knees to finish placing the highly polished baby blue rocks. A blue teddy bear held a large bouquet of yellow and white mini roses sprigged with baby's breath and blue ribbon, the final touch to her project and the finish of her life on this ranch.

She remained on her knees and patted the little mound of earth and stones. And then, for the first time since she had sold her home and felt so right about putting it all in her rear view mirror—she broke.

Despite the well-learned and practiced strength of her soul to accept her mistakes as part of living life on earth, she couldn't get there this time. She held her stomach with one hand while her other rested on the blurred swell of the small grave. She bent forward until her face nearly touched the rocks. Grief overwhelmed her, a crushing pain so intense, there was no help but to collapse inside and let herself finally know the loss of the only pure and innocent part of her. Her precious baby son.

She cried for him in a way she'd never cried before, feeling pain like she'd never felt before. When it consumed her, she screamed—and screamed.

Man-sized hands grasped her upper arms from behind and so slowly and gently pulled her up off of her knees and turned her around into strong arms that wrapped her tight against a broad familiar chest. She knew it was Les. But how? Why? And why now?

She trembled uncontrollably for several minutes, gasping for breath between the bone jarring sobs. Why now? Hysteria racked her. "Why now?" she screamed and jerked backward so hard, he was forced to loosen his grip. She began to push and pummel his chest, raging at the one she'd needed so desperately years ago, but he couldn't be found.

"Why are you here?" she screamed up at him as she pushed herself all the way out of his reach. "I needed you. *He* needed you."

"Katie?" He reached to take hold of her arms, but she backed up more.

"No!" Her sobs ebbed away and she stood now with her back against the fence railing, several feet from him.

Les stared at the pain in her face. It was heart wrenching. In the silence of the moment, his gaze moved from her face down to the beginning of a row of grave stones. The first one was her brother, *Jason Wade Grace.* He had stood at this graveside before. The next one was *Jason Lee Grace.* Kaitlyn's father. He didn't know he had died.

He looked back up at Kaitlyn. She was quietly watching him, her arms hanging by her sides.

Then he saw the blue and white mingled rocks on the last one. He realized a teddy bear was holding the bouquet of flowers and when his eyes traveled upward to read the name on the headstone, time stopped.

Daniel Les Kane.

Disbelief, panic, confusion. The date on the white marble—Les's mouth froze partially open, his watery eyes blurring the little mound in front of him. But he had read it. Read *his* name. *His* name. *His* baby.

When he finally turned his head to look at Kaitlyn, she was gone.

For several minutes, he stood still. He knew if he looked toward the house, he would see her walking, maybe running across the pasture. But he didn't look. He didn't move until his emotions were pulled back inside to a manageable level.

What had he done? The weight of his world, everything that encompassed his life, rested on his shoulders at that moment.   He raked both hands through his hair, his fingers laced and resting on top of his head. Almost immediately his hands fell back to hang at his sides, the weight riding his shoulders, too heavy.

Images of a young girl, a virgin, flirting her backside off and he'd taken what she offered without ever thinking of this possible consequence. He fell in love with her, yes, but he had left, swallowed up in his anger, leaving no clue how to find him. He had made her pregnant and left her to deal with—the loss of their baby.

He lowered his face and stared at the ground. She had tried to tell him. That night when she told him everything else, she said there was more, but he wouldn't let her tell him. This right here, this baby, he figured, had more to do with why she came looking for him than any of the rest of it.

He squatted down beside the little blue and white mound and ran his fingers over the name. *Daniel Les Kane.* How did she know? He hadn't told anyone that his first name was Daniel.

He calculated the date on the headstone and knew she had carried their baby for a little more than three months. Then he noticed the date on her father's stone. Jason died the same month Les had left for Wyoming.

He cursed himself for the pain and trauma he had unintentionally saddled on Katie by wallowing in his own selfish anger. And for how long? Years! And all the while, she was spending that same time, dealing with the loss of their baby, alone, dealing with the loneliness of having no family to help her grieve and living in a rehabilitation hospital for a full half year.

He left the cemetery and walked slowly across the field and around to the front door of the house. For the first time, he noticed the Realtor's sign in the front yard with a large lettered sign above it that said *Sold.* A car had been parked out there when he'd arrived. It must have blocked the sign from his view. Where was Kaitlyn planning to go?

The heavy front door was open, the storm door unlocked, so he went inside. Katie was sitting in an overstuffed recliner on the far side of the den. She didn't look at him, but stared at nothing in the space of the room. The storm inside of her had passed. The quiet seemed to comfort her. But to Les, it was suffocating. She looked so lost and forlorn.

As his gaze moved around the room, he noticed how empty the house looked. The furniture was here, but the walls were bare. Maybe they'd always been bare. This place just didn't look like Kaitlyn.

He crossed the room and squatted down beside her chair. He looked at her face, her eyes downcast. "I'm sorry, Katie. I'm sorry I wasn't here for you."

Without looking at him, she said softly, "It doesn't matter anymore. That's all past now. I wanted to tell you about Danny. I tried…"

"I know. I know you did."

They both spoke barely above a whisper.

"I'm…I'm honored that you gave him my name. You made him a junior, you know."

She attempted a slight smile. "Almost."

"No. For real. How did you know my first name is Daniel?"

Finally, she looked at him, eyes bright. "I didn't."

He matched her with a surprised glint. "Then, where did you get *Daniel* from?"

"The same place I found out he was a little boy. The night after my miscarriage, I dreamed about him. In the dream, I saw his name written on his grave marker. It was so clear. *Daniel Les Kane.* The doctor said it was too early to tell the sex, but I knew God had given me his name."

Les was amazed and humbled by her story. He ached to pull her up into his arms and hold her and love her, all the lost years worth.

"There's more, Les."

He waited, his hand gently clasping her forearm where it rested on the arm of the chair.

"I'm the reason our baby died. I didn't mean to, but I caused him to die." She paused, dry-eyed. "I hadn't slept in several nights and I was so exhausted...I took some over-the-counter sleeping pills. I lost him the next night."

Les's heart squeezed. "Katie, did the doctor tell you that's what happened?"

She shook her head slightly. "No. He called it an incompetent cervix. That sounded like I might have caused the incompetency."

"Katie, listen to me. No matter what anyone says happened, it's not going to make it better or understandable. You had to bury your first born son. No matter what the cause, it's not going to make that okay. But, I happen to know that a weakness in the cervix is a legitimate cause of miscarriage. It can usually be fixed with a minor surgery."

She didn't respond, other than a slight nod of her head.

"Katie, our baby is in God's Heaven. He's making out better than we are."

That brought a slight smile to her lips.

"And no matter what, I'll never hold you responsible for what happened. There is no fault here. But, if anybody is to blame for anything, it's me." Les reached up and took her face in his hands. "I came here to get you, Katie. To bring you back home with me. I want you to marry me. I love you. I always have."

He searched her face, her eyes that would tell him she needed and loved him. He could see she was vulnerable and afraid. He wanted more than anything to be the one to give her the love she'd been denied throughout her life. To fill in all the gaps left bleeding. He knew that was his place, his purpose in her life. He knew it deep inside of his bones.

Kaitlyn sucked a ragged breath. *Les.* He was everything she had dreamed about from the time she was a little girl—her prince on a white horse—someone to look at her the way he was looking at her now—to forgive her, even when she was such a screw up and to defend her, even when she was wrong.

But, every time that she believed a good thing had finally come her way because it felt good and looked good, it always crashed and burned right in front of her. She had no strength left to fight for this. Not anymore.

"I sold the ranch, Les. In a few days I'll be leaving. I have to go."

"Katie." Les pleaded for her to see his heart.

"Let me go, Les. Just let me go."

He sat on the side of his Holiday Inn bed in Joplin with his heart stuck down in his Justin boots. Nothing had prepared him for what he'd encountered today. He'd become a father years ago and never knew. But Kaitlyn's rejection when he had been so positive that she was in love with him was about to take him down.

Maybe this thing with Jesse wasn't as cut and dried as Jesse had made it sound. There *are* people with fickle hearts in this world—in love one day and then in love with another the next. But he knew that wasn't the truth about Katie. His pride had just taken another swift kick. That was all. He doubted if he would ever get over wondering where she had gone and if she was all right. His heart was going to ache for a long, long time.

But this time, something was different inside of him. He didn't feel the raging hate and bitterness he'd left here with under similar circumstances years ago. His concern then was only for himself. Not once had he checked to find out how Katie was during those years . It was always about him and his pain.

This time, he was hurting just as bad, but he was worried about her welfare. She had nobody and no place to go. There was so much meanness in the world now. How was she going to be safe? How was he going to be able to drive out of here tomorrow and leave her alone in the world? It felt like he would be leaving her for the wolves just by driving away. Tears dripped down his cheeks.

Bone of my bones, flesh of my flesh.

Oh, God, what can I do? Jesus, I need You to help me. I'm kind of new at praying to You, so, forgive me if I'm doing it wrong. But, I don't know how to just let her go like this. I love her. It's not right. If there's some way You can help me, well, I thank You.

Judd Luke kept popping through his mind. He couldn't seem to get rid of the thought of his boss until it registered that something must be up at the Double OO. He picked up the phone and got an outside line, then punched in the number. Judd picked up on the first ring.

"Hey, Les, how's it going?"

"It's not going. I'll be heading back in the morning. Everything all right up there?" His tone was blunt.

Judd heard it and paused several long seconds. "You want to talk about it, Les?"

He rubbed the back of his neck and twisted and turned, not use to whining about his problems like this. "I don't know, Judd." Then for the next fifteen minutes, he poured himself out to the preacher, not caring when his voice cracked or his tears flowed. "So, I don't know anything to do but head home."

"Let me ask a question and think about it before you answer. Is the Double OO truly home to you? Is this where you belong?"

Les was silent, slightly taken aback at the question. But after thinking good and long about it, he simply said, with strong conviction, "Yes, it is."

"Well, there's certainly no doubt in that answer."

"There is something I need to ask you before I hang up," Les said. "Jesse told me that God had put him and Laura together and it had something to do with a Bible verse that said *Bone of my bones, flesh of my flesh.*"

"That's right. We studied about that at church meeting a few months ago."

Les was quiet a while. Then, "I heard those words said, like, in my head, like they were spoken to me today. What does that mean, said to me like that?"

It was Judd's turn to be taken aback. Suddenly he knew exactly what to say to him. "Come home, Les. And I can, by the Spirit of God, Himself, give you this promise. If you and Kaitlyn are meant to be together by God's design, she'll come home to you. God will bring her."

Les wasn't reassured. He wanted so desperately to go get her and demand she come with him. But he knew that wouldn't be any good. He had no choice, but to go home.

The next morning, he headed out hours before sunup, taking a short detour. He carried a legal-sized envelope he had gotten from the motel clerk and a note to Katie sealed inside. What he had written was possibly going to be his last words to her—ever. He rolled down his window and slid it inside her mailbox on the road in front of her house.

With his heart pulled up out of his boots, it became lodged in his throat most of the way home.

The sun was barely streaking through the bedroom's east window. Kaitlyn's head ached, her eyes swollen until she could barely open them. She had cried all night.

She got up and went to the kitchen to swallow a couple of pain tablets, then padded back to bed. She propped herself up with pillows to give her stuffy nose a break.

Her whole life, such as it had been, was a past experience. It felt as though she was at an impasse. The old life, with everything that was still left in it, was tearing off of her so she could step into a new garment waiting to shroud her for another phase of life. Somehow, she knew this was what was happening. But the final tearing away of the *old* wasn't as hard to handle as the fact that Les wasn't to be included in whatever waited for her.

He had felt sorry for her. He blamed himself for what she'd been through. He had needed his guilt soothed, but she couldn't let him set them both up for any more unhappiness. She loved Les more than her own life. She could hardly stand the thought of living without him. But the old hurts would come back up between them. The past was best left there. Including Les. Wasn't he? Wasn't he?

"Oh, God. Oh, God." Fresh tears trickled. "Didn't I do everything You wanted. I forgave everybody. I read Your Bible. I prayed to You every day." She squeezed her eyes shut a moment against the intense throbbing in the top of her head. She forced herself to relax and breathe. After a few minutes, the pain ebbed away and a sweet calm enveloped her. "If you'll tell me what You want from me, Lord, I'll do it. I'll do it for You."

All of the racking heartache that had spun her out of control all night long and brought on the worst headache she'd ever had, was suddenly soothed over with a sweet covering of some sort. Something almost silky-feeling wrapped her entire being, something not of this earth.

She realized at that moment that her Lord Jesus was truly first in her life. For the first time since she got home, she felt a smile on the inside of her.

A week later, her car was loaded with only her clothes and other personal effects. Everything left in the house now belonged to the new ranch owners. She'd had her mail delivery sent to a post office box since the day the ranch sold. There wasn't much mail anyway, just a few bills which she had already taken care of. Her good-bye was said at the family cemetery early that morning.

With her purse and little red journal in the bucket seat beside her, she drove down the driveway without a glance back.

Until that moment, she had not allowed a hint of fear to slow her down. But suddenly, there it was, moving over her before she could stop it. She stopped her car at the end of the driveway and threw it in park. Not one small clue had entered her head about where she was going.

Of all times, at this moment, she realized what an idiotic thing she was doing. She had asked God for a direction, but now that she had a brain cell hitting a cylinder, she realized He had never answered her. That was a week ago and she had run around closing up her life and now, driving away without a clue one. The past week had felt so right and purposed. Now she just felt foolish and lame.

She got out of her car and leaned against the front fender, her arms indignantly folded across her chest. "Well, Lord." She began angrily patting one foot on the ground. "This is a *fine* howdy do! You can be speaking to me anytime now. I mean, I don't even know which way to turn my car wheels! Left? Right?"

Just then, her eye landed on her abandoned mailbox. It was shut! She *always* left it open and the mail person *always* closed it when mail was put in it. That had long been the habit. "That's just great! An overdue bill, probably," she muttered as she stomped over and yanked open the door. She pulled out a white envelope and flipped it over to view the front of it.

She thought her heart had stopped when she saw *Kaitlyn* written largely across it in Les's handwriting. She blinked and stared at it for a long time.

Slowly, she walked back and got in her car. With shaky hands, she opened it. On the single sheet of paper inside, she read:

Bone of my bones, flesh of my flesh
Together forever, Les

Her whole body was trembling now. She reached for her journal, opened the back cover and read the words she'd heard in Les's kitchen that day. *Bone of my bones, flesh of my flesh.*

She reread Les's paper, then her journal.

"Lord?" Her eyes filled. She knew.

Go home, child.

In three days it would be Christmas. Les thought the lonely days since his return from Joplin was going to break him. He had lived out on the range in Judd's tent, refusing to dirty up the house. He'd gone in to shower and do laundry, but couldn't bear to be there without Katie.

He had learned to pray a little better. At least, he was doing a lot of it, and was happy to learn that the prayers for Ms.

Martha Walton had been answered. She would recover from her minor stroke. Judd had spent a few hours in the tent with him, teaching him things about God and keeping enough hope in him to keep him sane. Not necessarily that Katie would ever come home to him, but that God had a good plan for him and would lead him into it if he kept trusting Him to do it.

Les had steer-wrestled some really bad boys out here on this range, was gored in the ribs and kicked in really *rude places.* All of that was as easy as eating a bag of popcorn, compared to living this Christian way. But Something just wouldn't let him give it up. The past couple of days were almost unbearable. He'd already made up his mind to let Christmas come and go without him.

Judd and Toni always made a big splash for the whole ranch crew at Christmas every year—big turkey and dressing dinner with all the trimmings and gifts. He always tried to avoid the whole thing, but the Luke's wouldn't hear of it.

But this year, he was going to sleep that day away in this tent. He was drained, emotionally and physically. His trust in God was weakening. He didn't know how to keep believing for something that he thought should have already happened.

Katie would have gotten her mail that same day he'd left her the note. She never responded. Maybe she didn't understand it and threw it away.

He'd swallowed so many throat lumps and threatening tears for many nights now. But, tonight this tent seemed lonelier than ever. It was like a knife twisting inside him. Is this what God does to a cowboy after he makes a fool of himself over

Him? Sticks his butt in a tent on the back ninety of nowhere and leaves him like he was being punished?

He didn't seem to have had a choice in running to the preacher that night. Judd told him he had made a right *choice* in giving his life to Jesus. But it felt more like he'd been jerked up out of this tent and driven like a prisoner to Judd's front porch and thrown against the doorbell, over and over. Guess God was afraid he might escape when he took off for Joplin, because here he is, back in the tent, worse than before.

Judd had explained when he'd rode out here the last time, that God was just needing him to learn to trust Him. Only Him! Well, who *else* did God think he was going to trust? There wasn't anybody *else* for acres around!

Les finished his pity party and felt bad for it. He repented, ate his peanut butter and jelly sandwich he had brought from home the day before and laid back on his clean smelling blankets. At least he had washed the nasty things a few days ago. It was barely dark-thirty, but he was tired and he didn't want to think anymore.

"Hey, Les?" Judd shot the beam from his flashlight right into Les's eyes. That was about the only part of him showing under the quilt that had wrapped him up like an enchilada. "Boy, you better be getting up from there and ready for my wife's big Christmas shindig. She'll be up here after you herself if you don't."

Les was awake, but didn't open his eyes. He'd heard the whining diesel dually coming a half mile out. Finally, when the light stayed stuck to his lids, he sat up and squinted at his watch around his wrist.

"It's 6 o'clock. You better get a move on. I assure you, you *don't* want *her* coming up here."

"Aw, Judd. Tell her, I'm sorry. I'm tired and I already ate a sandwich. I didn't know the party was tonight." The last thing Les thought he could endure right now was a party. He wanted to sleep until the holiday cheer was over.

"No can do, cowboy. Roll out." Judd grabbed the edge of the blanket and jerked, flipping Les like a hot cake, except he felt like a Popsicle. "I don't know why you haven't froze to death yet."

"Me either."

"Go on home and get a shower. You stink." Judd turned off the flashlight, walked out and left.

"Yeah, okay. I don't know who you smell," Les mumbled into the dark space. "I had a shower. A man can't have a decent gloomy night of depression around here." He moaned to his feet and stretched. He guessed he could suck it up one more Christmas.

Judd's truck lights had already disappeared by the time Les backed out and headed for home. The truck bounced over the rise into the space where his cabin came into view.

His throat constricted when he saw the multicolored Christmas lights twinkling across his front porch railing and down the length of the log columns. He let the truck coast to a stop about even with the pond, his heart racing at the sight of a small Christmas tree glittering through his front window. The lamps were all glowing in the den, too.

The tail lights of Judd's truck had stopped moving just before he would have rounded the bend of trees, headed toward his home. That's when Les caught sight of Judd standing outside by his tailgate and waving. He was saying goodnight.

The little black Camry was pulled up and half hidden on the side of the house.

The strongest emotion that had ever passed through Les at one time was all over him now. "Lord?" He wondered almost audibly how God could keep on being Good and Kind to him when he wanted to throw Him under a stampede in his fits of anger.

My Mercy Endures Forever!

Les parked beside the pond, got out and walked toward the house. He had to work at breathing normally. Before he reached the front porch, he smelled the cookies baking.

The front door opened and Kaitlyn walked out. She was dressed in faded denim wranglers with the rounded toes of equally well-worn Roper boots slightly showing. Her red plaid, long sleeved over-shirt was tied up at the waist and showing a long white fitted ribbed T underneath. Her sleeves were rolled up and a long wooden spoon was in her hand.

When Les saw her, he thought he would choke to death on the big gulp of air he inhaled. They stood still a minute and drank from the twinkling sparks they were exchanging.

"I like what you've done with the place," he said, his eyes fixed on hers.

"Thanks. It *is* Christmas, you know."

He nodded and took a slow step toward her, and then another, until he stood inches away, looking up at her where she stood on the edge of the porch.

"I was just curious about something," she stated quietly.

"What's that?"

"Am I the bones...or the flesh?"

Les threw his head back and laughed with pure joy. "I haven't got a clue, but if I had to guess, I'd say our bones and flesh are a perfect match." He caught her around her waist and swung her up and out until she squealed like a trapped rabbit. When he let her feet touch the ground, he wrapped her up in a grizzly-bear hug and held on for dear life—for a long time.

He finally pulled back enough to share with her in a long, deep kiss that confirmed their new beginning.

His attention was drawn toward the house a moment, and then he hugged her tight again. With his mouth against her ear and a grin across his face, he whispered, "Your cookies are burning."

****

PREVIEW OF

BOOK FOUR IN THE

SURRENDERED SERIES

SURRENDERED IV

FOREVER

PREVIEW

The group reached the creek crossing below the cave just steps behind Andy. He could tell the water was closer to normal and never slowed down when he got to the bank.

They all plowed across the, not quite knee deep, flow, but when Andy grasped a tree limb to begin pulling himself up the cliff, Jesse grasped his arm.

"Whoa, Andy. What are you doing?" He was afraid his son was hurt and not thinking clear.

"The cave is up there, Dad." He reared back and pointed straight up.

They all stared upward, almost the same dumbfounded expression coating each of their faces. Nobody moved until Andy dropped his blanket wrap and vanished up the slick side winding trail.

Les Kane was the last to be helped over the top of the ledge before they all rushed inside the wide opening of the cave.

They found Andy standing a couple of steps from the girl as if frozen in place.

It was Les who reacted after the first initial shock loosened that had struck the whole atmosphere inside the cavern. It didn't matter that he was a veterinarian. His doctor's instinct rushed him to her side and checked first for a pulse. He couldn't find it.

Judd went to his knees beside Les and began to pray quietly for the girl's life. Kaitlyn gasped and knelt beside Judd, silently joining his prayer.

Reeny's small body was partly curled in a fetal position. Her long blonde waves splayed over her face and across her bare arms like thick silken strings. She only wore a thin long sleeved T-shirt, her knit jogging pants pulled down to her knees. Mud and blood lumped together on her clothes and the ground around her. A dirty blanket was grasped within the furl of her body, her arms pulling it close for extra warmth. A second blanket lay wadded at her feet.

Les twisted around just enough to take stock of where everyone was. Jesse stood rigid and unreadable several feet behind them. Andy was on the opposite side of the enclosure moving something around.

"Katy, go see about Andy." Les ordered.

She immediately got up and noticed Andy piling wood on what had been a campfire. She went to help and by the time she gathered what was left of sticks and driftwood, a fire blazed behind her. She turned and looked at Andy. He was staring into the flickering blaze, his eyes brimming in silent pain. This young boy was in such turmoil. What he must have experienced tonight that no child should have.

She dropped her offering close to the fire circle and went to him to put an arm around his shoulders.

"You did a good job tonight, honey. The best anyone could do in these circumstances," she whispered against his ear. "It'll be okay. God's got this."

His shoulders shook as the hot anguish spilled over and dripped off of his chin. He heard her words and understood them, but they didn't penetrate deep enough to bring relief to his little boy soul. He knew Reeny was dead. He had been the only hope she and her baby had and he failed. Andy's heart was broken in a way he hadn't been aware existed. He felt like curling up beside Reeny and going with her. But he just stood still and cried.

Les had sent Katy away for her own sake, before he gently took the blanket that Reeny's lifeless arms held. He knew there would be a tiny body hidden under the folds. It's umbilical cord was still attached to its mother.

Even though it had been a few years ago, Kaitlyn had given birth to their son too early and blamed her own negligence for his death. The last time she had spoken of their baby, she cried. He wanted to spare her this.

Les quickly cut the cord with his pocket knife, tied it off and gently wrapped the deceased infant girl. He believed the baby had been stillborn. Judd Luke took the bundle and held it close, willing the cold little baby to feel his love.

Les continued to search for a pulse in the mother. She had lost a lot of blood, but her color was still good. He turned her flat on her back and began CPR. That's when a second pair of hands appeared to lay on the girl's chest. Les cut his eyes up at Jesse and nodded his head.

The pair worked together for what seemed forever, before finally deciding it was useless. Les reached and took Jesse's hand over the top of the girl's body and said a prayer that she would live forever with Him.

The two men stood up, both with tears spilling over, as Judd lay his tiny bundle in the crook of Reeny's arm. No one spoke or moved. No one could.

The still silence in that place had become thick, almost like a cloud had come in and was holding them all in a frozen trance. It was a peaceful feeling. This moment belonged to the mother and child lying on the ground. They all knew it and stood respectfully reticent.

www.ingramcontent.com/pod-product-compliance
Lightning Source LLC
Chambersburg PA
CBHW022017170626
46808CB00001B/458